The Sea of Azov

The Sea
of Azov

Stories by *Amy Bloom, Ellen Galford, Tania Hershman, Zvi Jagendorf, Etgar Keret, Nicole Krauss, Shaun Levin, Karen Maitland, Jon McGregor, Eshkol Nevo, Ali Smith, Michelene Wandor, Jonathan Wilson, Tamar Yellin, Richard Zimler.*

Foreword by *Anne Sebba.*

Edited by Anne Joseph

www.fiveleaves.co.uk

The Sea of Azov

Published in 2009 by Five Leaves,
PO Box 8786, Nottingham NG1 9AW
(www.fiveleaves.co.uk)
in association with World Jewish Relief
(www.wjr.org.uk)

ISBN: 978 1 905512 60 7 (pbk)
978 1 905512 61 4 (hbk)

Five Leaves acknowledges financial support
from Arts Council England

Five Leaves is a member of Inpress
(www.inpressbooks.co.uk),
representing individual publishers

Design and typesetting: Four Sheets Design and Print
Printed in Great Britain

Contents

Introduction
Anne Joseph

Founded in 1933 World Jewish Relief, www.wjr.org.uk, formally known as CBF — the Central British Fund for German Jewry, was the organisation that instigated the Kindertransport, which brought 10,000, mainly Jewish children, to the UK from Nazi Europe. Nowadays it is the leading overseas aid arm of the UK Jewish community, providing basic welfare support in the form of food, medication and fuel, primarily but not exclusively, to Jewish communities in need around the world. It also assists in sustaining and renewing Jewish life in these communities, enabling them to thrive. Much of this work is carried out in the former Soviet Union, Bulgaria, Serbia and Argentina. Additionally, WJR channels the UK Jewish community's response to global disasters such as the crises in Darfur and Burma.

Within WJR various committees operate, one of which is CONNECTIONS. Launched in 1990 by a group of women dedicated to playing a part in the challenging rebirth of Jewish life in Eastern Europe, their energies have been focused towards supporting Jewish students in the Former Yugoslavia — students who could not have continued their studies without their help. Funds are raised primarily via an Annual Musical Evening, through a variety of literary events as well as by sponsorship of individuals.

WJR is always looking for creative ways of raising its profile as well as funds for its humanitarian work. About eighteen months ago Ardyn Halter, an Israeli based artist friend of several CONNECTIONS committee members, came up with the idea of publishing a collection of short stories around the theme of "connections."

My involvement with WJR came about quite naturally. My grandparents had been recipients of CBF assistance. I had been looking for ways to get involved with the charity so when Linda Rosenblatt, Vice-chair of WJR, mentioned that a book of short stories had been mooted as a possible project, I, a freelance editor, jumped at the opportunity and set the project in motion. In keeping with the charity's philosophy of working within the global community it was decided that we would include stories written by both Jewish and non-Jewish authors. Each story had to be between 2000-5000 words, the theme of connection being the only criterion. When Five Leaves Publications agreed to publish the book what had started as a possibility became a reality. Some authors have written stories specifically for *The Sea of Azov*, others gave permission to reprint their work. Additionally there are a few stories that are making their debut in English. It is a diverse collection for a remarkable charity, whose work is as vital now as it always was.

8

Foreword
Anne Sebba

There's a party game I remember playing as a child which had long lingering effects. Everyone secretly wrote down their birth dates on a piece of paper, then folded this up while another person (an adult of course) predicted that two would fall on the same date and tried to pick out who the "twins" were.

I was always stunned by the result. But the coincidence which linked these two people together was not really so surprising. Mathematicians tell us that among a group of 23 people there is a 50% likelihood of two sharing a birth date. There is, after all, only a finite number of days from which to choose.

Biographers, and I am one, crave connections to the subjects they are exploring. It's necessary to elevate ourselves from the level of vulture seeking blood and guts. It's part of the proof we seek that there is a reason for us to be writing a particular book. Yet worlds collide so readily that it sometimes seems we are trying too hard. For example, my last two biographies (Jennie Churchill and William Bankes) have had both a connecting date and a connecting name: April 15th was the date that William Bankes, the exiled collector, died in 1855, and the same date that Jennie Jerome married Randolph Churchill in 1874. It was also the date my mother died in 1993 so a special date for me. When I looked further I discovered that Rosetta was my mother's middle name, William Bankes was involved in deciphering the Rosetta Stone and Randolph proposed to Jennie at Rosetta Cottage on the Isle of Wight three days after they met. The cottage still stands and I have sat under its roof, making a connection with my subject.

Laura Ashley, the subject of a previous biography of mine, died on her birth date, as did William Shakespeare a few centuries earlier. Winston Churchill died on the same date that his father died. How significant are any of these connections? Or, are they all just examples of the giant random coincidence that is life itself, in the midst of which is death?

And yet. And yet. They do matter as we all search for a meaning in life. It's the park bench syndrome. It's the reason we give our children significant names redolent of family ancestry, or write our memoirs. It's the means of ensuring we are remembered by our friends or descendants. Most of us yearn to understand why we are here, to make a difference while we are here in an attempt to secure our place for posterity. You only have to stand outside the National Archives in Kew to see thousands of people each week longing to discover the roots of their family tree to explain their place on the branches and see what sort of fruit they will leave behind.

And so I read these stories certain that I would find connections between them and there are plenty. Whispers and shadows abound. The dark menace lurking in the best fairy tales is never far from the surface in most of these stories too. All the contributors, whatever differences in age, gender or geographical location, are trying to make sense of the brutal century from which we have emerged and the uncertain one into which we are still tentatively trespassing, not ready to claim ownership. Some have sought connections to dead relatives who live on in memory or genetic inheritance.

Ellen Galford, in her captivating time travel story, pushes this idea to its limits as she tells how the boy Alex goes off to be an assistant to the prophet Jeremiah in old Judea.

Richard Zimler, in his extraordinarily powerful story, describes his father's decline into an Alzheimerish haze. At times the old man was convinced he was being dunked underwater by a Cossack marauder or that his entire village of Jews was being butchered.

"As we reach the end of our lives," asks Zimler, "Do we all return to our ancestral landscape? Will I, too, return to the threatening forests of Poland even though I've never set foot inside that country?"

But here is the conundrum: do Jews from different lands — Diaspora Jews — have stronger connections than, say, Diaspora Catholics or Diaspora Palestinians? Or is it just that we search harder for them? I am not going to dwell on these arguably accidental connections. After all, as Zimler's protagonist makes plain, we are each individuals with vitally different stories, even (or perhaps especially), different from our own siblings. Better that the reader discovers these for his or herself, connections the authors may not have intended.

The first short stories I treasured were by Anton Chekhov. Chekhov trained as a medical student but started winning prizes for his stories almost immediately. Chekhov is the master of the genre; he distils what it is that makes us both human and barbarian, what it is that makes us alive and want to assert our aliveness. His writing covers the full range of emotions and he is as comfortable pinning loss to the page as he is betrayal and fear, in revealing desire and satisfaction, love, grief and revenge.

Chekhov was born in 1860 in a port on the Sea of Azov in Southern Ukraine. There has been a Jewish presence in Ukraine since the 10th century and a particularly vibrant cultural life existed there in the 19th and early 20th centuries. But the Cossacks inflicted terrible punishments in regular pogroms on the Jews and, although there were no concentration camps within Ukraine itself, one of the worst massacres of the entire war took place on Ukrainian soil.

The Sea of Azov provided my connection to this book. Today the sea lies within the borders of The Russian Federation and Ukraine, the latter independent since 1991 and enjoying a flourishing economy, but scarred with pockets of dreadful poverty as well. It's where, as a journalist, I first came across World Jewish Relief in action, teams of people who provide a lifeline in the form of food, medicine and human contact to those who may have a long standing link to the land but a pretty tenuous hold on life itself. It's also where I had a meeting with a man who deepened my shallow understanding of what fighting for life really means.

Grigory Rodin now lives in a one room flat in Berdyansk on the Sea of Azov, with his wife. I was a stranger who walked into his life with an interpreter one summer's day. Yet he told me, straightforwardly, of the day in 1941, after the Germans invaded his home town of Kiev, when he went searching for his parents. He never found them but was pushed into line and marched towards a local ravine, a beauty spot: Babi Yar, the name now synonymous with the murder of 34,000 Jews in two days.

When he finally reached the pit he was so afraid he just remembers feeling a terrible pain in my face where he had been shot. Luckily the bullet only grazed his cheek — he showed me the scar — and then he lost consciousness and fell in.

Sixty years later Rodin still has nightmares about that day; the weight of bodies all around, under and on top of him, the stench of blood and the visceral fear. But as guards were patrolling around he stifled his screams, eventually managing to crawl out of the pit and hide in a nearby cemetery.

Grigory Rodin spent the rest of the war living rough, just surviving. Eventually he reached Stalingrad, where he found work in a factory. Now in poor health with few resources to support him, he depends on the daily visits from World Jewish Relief.

As a biographer I am constantly forced to question the morality (and possibility) of compressing a life into 400 pages. But perhaps the greater truth is to be found in 40 or even 4 pages, in an episode, in a look. After all every writer is searching for a version of the truth, sometimes one that is more reliable than memory. But sometimes less.

Eshkol Nevo writes in his poignant fragment of a childhood memory: "At the moment the truth is stronger than me." But, knowing that we all see different images even in a mirror, is it the truth we are seeing or a reflection of it that pleases us? As I read Tamar Yellin's chilling piece another childhood activity came back to me; I used to love scratching the black from behind my mother's small handbag mirrors. But it wasn't really glass that remained, not a glass that you could see through. Just a no-good mirror where the reflection never pleased me.

As writers perhaps we cannot avoid lying with every sentence we create as we seek to embellish the half remembered truth, to retell the familiar tale and shape it into the form that suits our current purpose. But if Memory is to be our guide to the past, we owe a duty to the future to ensure that he leads us by the straightest path.

Or, as Ali Smith points out in the pages that follow:

"When is the short story like a nymph? When the echo of it answers back."

Read these and listen for the echo!

Richmond 2008

Mother's Day

Karen Maitland

A thousand tiny cruelties swarm around death; phantasms so insubstantial that they do not even own a form, much less a name. Wisps of memories, transparent and fragile as a spider's web, lurk behind every cupboard door or drawn curtain. They crouch in the dusty corners, waiting, watching. A breath of song, a whisper of lilac, a shadow in a chair — surely these ghostly echoes can cause no hurt to the living, but they do, believe me, they do.

During those first three weeks after her mother died, it seemed to Ruth that the whole house was laying traps for her. Just when she thought she was getting a grip of herself, as friends told her she must for little Bethany's sake, she would blunder into something else that made her tears well up all over again. They were silly inconsequential things; the waft of her mother's gardenia soap from the faded silk dressing gown; the little heap of ivory face powder spilt in the corner of a drawer; the softly curled grey hairs caught in the bristles of the ancient Mason Pearson hairbrush.

Ruth could arm herself to cope with the planned events, the funeral and the will, registering the death and reading the condolence cards, but these tiny half-remembrances sprang at her without warning and always found her defenceless.

The worst was the post which came dropping unbidden through her door: the cheerful postcard to her mother from a friend on a winter cruise; the letter inviting her mother to apply for life insurance; the bill from the newsagents demanding money for papers her mother would never read. But on that Monday morning in late November, it was not a letter addressed to her mother that made Ruth's stomach lurch, it was a letter addressed to Ruth herself.

The white envelope lay stiff upon the mat covering the *wel* of *welcome*. Ruth stood gazing down at it, unable to move; even her breath was frozen in her chest. The grandfather clock in the hall ticked off its hollow minutes, but Ruth could not bring herself to touch the envelope. Only when the clock began to strike eleven did the sound jerk her out of her shock and she finally stooped to pick up the letter. She carried it into the kitchen, laying it in the middle of the scrubbed wooden table. She sank onto a stool, staring at it, her hands clamped tightly under her thighs as if her fingers might betray her and open the letter before she had time to prepare herself.

She knew the handwriting better than her own, a firm distinct copperplate, written with a worn fountain pen in turquoise ink. The pen which had addressed the envelope and the bottle of turquoise ink were still lying in her mother's writing desk upstairs where they had been kept ever since Ruth could remember.

Once, when she was a child, Ruth had tiptoed into her mother's bedroom whilst she was in the garden, desperate to explore the treasures hidden in the doll-sized drawers of the desk. With one tiny finger she had caressed the red and gold leather stamp-case, the letter-opener shaped like a toy sword and the enchanting glass bottle of ink with its silver top. Struggling to open the bottle, she had spilled a little of the ink on the shell-pink carpet. She never dared touch that desk again, for her mother had used the Mason Pearson hairbrush hard on Ruth's bare bottom and even after all these years Ruth was not able to approach the desk without a flush of guilt and dread. Just staring at the ink on that white envelope was enough to make her face burn again from the memory.

But the letter could not be from her mother. She was dead; she'd died in a packed hospital ward. She'd never regained consciousness from the blood clot she suffered two days after her hip operation. The nurse had assured Ruth it was a blessing.

"Swift and painless, dear, always the best way. You wouldn't want her to linger, not if she was paralysed. Some poor souls don't even know their own families after a stroke. You wouldn't wish that on her, dear, now would you?"

No, this letter must be from a distant relative, someone of her mother's age. Most children of that generation had been drilled in the same neat handwriting and many had never lost the art.

Ruth snatched up the envelope, and ripping the top, pulled out a single sheet of thick cream paper.

Darling Ruth,

Please remember to plant up the hyacinth bulbs in the pots ready for early flowering and put them in the airing cupboard until the first shoots appear. Do not overwater. The compost should be moist, not wet.

Fondest love,
Mother

Ruth's throat was so tight, she thought she would choke. She glanced at the top of the letter. It was undated. Her mother must have written it in hospital the night before her operation. It was typical of her to worry about something as trivial as hyacinth bulbs, when most people would have been thinking only of their surgery. Ruth found the tears running down her cheeks at the sudden realisation that her mother would never again smell the sweetness of hyacinths.

But why had the letter taken over three weeks to arrive? Probably it had been left in her mother's locker or had fallen behind it, and a cleaner had only just found it. You were always reading in the papers about how infrequently wards were cleaned. It was outrageous, sheer incompetence. The letter might have been important. She ought to complain, though she knew she wouldn't. Suppose the cleaner got the sack; she couldn't live with the guilt of that.

Ruth rubbed savagely at her raw red eyes. Then she tucked the letter inside one of her mother's gardening books on the shelf, where she couldn't stumble across it again by accident. Bulbs, yes, Mother, I'll plant up the bulbs for you. Bethany and I can do it together when she comes home from school, a bit of quality mum-and-daughter time.

There hadn't been much of that these last two years, not since they had moved in with Mother. Mother said it was the ideal arrangement; she needed someone to look after her, and Ruth needed a roof over head now that good-for-nothing husband of hers had finally done the decent thing and left her. Besides with little Bethany starting school in a year, Ruth would need something to occupy her days. Mother had always made sure that Ruth's days were fully occupied.

All through her childhood and teenage years, there had been just the two of them. Ruth did not remember her father. He had died before she was two years old, suffocated by a leaky gasfire, a tragic accident. A neighbour had once shown Ruth the yellowed clipping from the local paper. Just four lines, that was all his life and death had amounted to.

There were no photographs of him in the house, no photographs of anyone. "Clutter," Mother called them. "Only sit around gathering dust. No point in keeping photos; what will they mean to anyone after I'm gone?"

Everyone constantly told Ruth that she should try to be an especially good girl for her poor widowed mother and she had tried, she really had, not least because the price of disobedience was her mother's silence, the tight-lipped banging down of plates, the audible sighs, proclaiming how deep was the wound of having born a thankless child. Guilt could smart more fiercely than any hairbrush.

★★★

Ruth had slipped quietly back into the routine of the house as if the years with Mike had never happened. There was only little Bethany to remind her of him, but she had inherited her grandmother's chestnut eyes and softly curling hair. The older Bethany grew, the less Ruth could see of Mike in her, until she could see nothing of him in the child at all. Bethany never asked about her dad. Mother never spoke his name and Ruth was kept far too busy to have time to grieve for the death of his love. Perhaps that was part of Mother's plan. As she always said, like any good mother, she'd only ever wanted what was best for her daughter.

Mother wasn't an invalid. She was quite capable of shopping, cooking and even light cleaning. But the day Ruth moved back in, her mother had retired from all housework, though not from issuing orders. Ruth tried not to resent it. After all, her mother was giving them a home and a home had to be polished and cleaned, dusted and scrubbed. Her mother had impressed that on Ruth from the moment she could toddle. It was a fulltime occupation, three hundred and sixty-five days of the year, to keep even a modest semi spotless. Her mother waged an unceasing war on the cohorts of dirt and dust and their attendant legions of smells and germs. Relax your guard for a single hour and slovenliness and filth would run rampant through the house.

But the days were never long enough, and the tasks never carried out well enough to meet her mother's exacting standards. Little Bethany was often rushed through her dinner, eaten alone in the kitchen so she didn't drop crumbs on the carpet, before being sent to play quietly in her bedroom and finally hustled to bed, without Ruth ever finding the time to read her a bedtime story or listen to what she had done at school.

But all that would change now. True, the last three weeks had seemed busier than ever, with the funeral to arrange, solicitors to be contacted, officials to be notified and papers to be signed, but now things were beginning to settle down and Bethany would have her undivided attention from now on. She deserved that, poor kid.

***

It was exactly a week later when the second letter arrived.

> *Darling Ruth,*
>
> *You must remember to make up a box for the Orphans in Romania Appeal. I always send one every year and they will be expecting it. Do not leave it until it is too late as you usually do.*
>
> *Fondest love,*
> *Mother*

As Ruth read the list of what the box should contain, she was not crying this time; she was shaking violently. Another letter found behind a locker? Surely hospital cleaners could not be that slipshod. But perhaps this letter had been given to a nurse to post and the woman had forgotten it until she came across it at the bottom of a capacious handbag or stuffed in the pocket of a seldom-worn coat. That was possible, wasn't it?

When the third envelope arrived, even Ruth could not convince herself that these were letters someone had neglected to post.

> *Darling Ruth,*
>
> *Do stop Bethany from biting her nails, it is a very ugly habit and one she will regret if allowed to continue. You must buy some bitter aloes and paint them on her nails before bed and again before school, as I used to do for you. You must also tie cotton gloves on her hands before she goes to bed.*

Ruth rang the solicitor — had her mother given them a stack of letters to post one at a time?

Of course not, the solicitor told her indignantly. No respectable firm would dream of doing such a thing. If she was receiving offensive or threatening mail then it was a matter for the police or she could take out an injunction against the sender, to prevent any further contact.

Could you take out an injunction against the dead? Ruth was pretty sure you couldn't and anyway, what grounds would she have? A judge would hardly regard notes about planting bulbs or biting nails as threatening.

★★★

Bethany tugged at her skirt. "Mummy, who are you hiding from?"

Ruth had taken to hovering behind the curtain of the sitting-room window peering out at the driveway as the hands

21

of the clock edged towards eleven. That was when the postman came and she couldn't bear the agony of listening for the plop of letters falling onto the mat. At least if she watched him coming up the street, she'd have a few minutes warning to prepare herself.

Distracted for a moment by her little daughter, Ruth glanced away from the window and too late heard the letters flop onto the mat. Before Ruth could stop her, Bethany ran down the hall and in seconds she was back, thrusting the letters into her mum's hand.

Ruth's stomach knotted as she flicked through the envelopes. Only bills, thank heaven. She felt the tightness in her chest ease just a little. Maybe there wouldn't be any more letters.

"Mummy, you're all shivery. Are you cold? Shall I get your cardigan?"

"No, angel. I just need a nice warm hug."

Ruth laid her cheek against Bethany's dark hair. Then she recoiled, staring down at the child. She shuddered violently before she could even name the alien scent which hung about her. She had always adored the smell of her daughter's skin. It had hardly changed since she was a baby, a comforting yeasty smell. But this wasn't the scent of her own little daughter; it was an adult smell… gardenia.

She held Bethany away from her. "Have you been using Grandma's soap?"

The child shook her head. "Princess sparkly soap."

It was true, Ruth had seen her wash her face with it not an hour ago. It smelt like tinned strawberries and had glittery particles embedded it, which was why Bethany insisted on it. Besides, Ruth had given all the unopened boxes of gardenia soap to a charity shop, unable to bear the reminder of the smell. Where would Bethany have got hold of it? The child

22

must have been playing in Grandma's room; the perfume still lingered faintly in there. Ruth sniffed again, but the smell had dissolved.

★★★

Monday morning came again too quickly and with it another envelope bearing the familiar inscription.

> *Darling Ruth,*
> *Please ensure you vacuum every carpet twice daily, once against the pile and the second time with the pile, otherwise the dirt will work deep into the carpet and it will become matted. I know you think that vacuuming once only will do very well, but the damage will soon become evident.*

Ruth rang every name in her mother's address book — did my mother leave some letters for you to post?

"No, dear. Have you lost some? Are you sure you're feeling quite well... you don't sound it..."

Ruth stared again at the letter in her hand. There was something not quite right about this handwriting. She took down the gardening book and pulled out the earlier letters, laying them side by side with this latest one. The writing was different on this one, but she had seen it before.

She hurried into the kitchen and rummaged in the drawer of the bleached-white table until she found the battered exercise book. It was a collection of recipes that her mother had copied out in her domestic science lessons when she was at senior school. The writing was neat, elegant and textbook perfect, lacking the individual character that age would bring to her handwriting. This last letter, though unmistakeably still in her mother's graceful copperplate, was in exactly the same hand as the recipes in the

23

book, as if it had been written by her mother when she was a young woman.

★★★

The letters continued to arrive with a chilling regularity, like a constantly dripping tap. They say you get used to that echoing rhythm after a time, but you don't, not when each icy drop is pounding hard on raw skin.

> *You will find the packets of seeds inside the brown teapot in the garden shed, the one you carelessly cracked when you were nine.*

The postmark was always too blurred to read, the letters undated. Ruth had given up trying to trace their source. Only a mother could know such secrets about her child.

> *You are too old to wear that shade of red lipstick. It is the same one you used to smuggle out of the house when you were on your way to meet that young tearaway, even though you swore to me were going the library to study for your exams. The lipstick looked cheap on you then and looks even more vulgar now.*

Ruth considered not opening the letters, burning them as soon as they arrived, but she couldn't bring herself to do it. It was as impossible as putting the phone down on her mother when she was alive. She'd fantasised about doing that many times when she was living with Mike, but there was always the fear that if she did, her mother might materialise in person on her doorstep and there'd be no cutting her off in mid sentence then.

There was only one solution, she and Bethany must leave the house. That was the only way to put a stop to this daily torment. They'd move far away, not leaving a forwarding address. The letters couldn't follow her then. She could even change her name. The papers were full of stories of people who had done that to cover their tracks. A fresh start might be just what she and Bethany needed. But she'd have to sell the house first. She'd need the money; without it she would never be able to afford a mortgage. She couldn't even raise enough for a deposit on a rented property.

But as the solicitor explained, in a patronizingly patient tone, the house wasn't hers to sell. Her mother had left everything in trust to Bethany, to prevent any possibility of Ruth's absent husband making a claim on it. And as a trustee of the estate, the solicitor would not contemplate a sale.

"I could only agree to it, if it were in the child's best interests and with the house prices falling, this would be the worst possible time to put a property on the market. Besides, my dear, why should you want to move? It's a perfectly delightful little house. Your late mother maintained it beautifully and it's so convenient for young Bethany's school."

★★★

Even before she'd remembered what it was she was dreading, Ruth found herself waking each morning with a feeling that she was drowning in a bottomless pool of tar. As the days past, she could feel herself sinking deeper into the smothering ooze of it, unable to run, unable to free herself.

She'd watch for the postman obsessively, refusing to stir from the window, praying that this morning he would walk straight past the house. She counted the cars — if there were three blue ones in a row and there would be no letter. If there were five starlings on the lawn the letter wouldn't come. The steel band around her chest would tighten and tighten as the ebony hands of the clock in the hall inched closer and closer towards eleven. If the postman was late, the pounding in Ruth's chest and the cold sweat creeping down between her breasts, was so unbearable that she wanted to run out of the house to confront him wherever he was and snatch the letters from his hand, but she didn't. And still the letters came.

> *Darling Ruth,*
>
> *How could you even think of selling my home? You should be thankful, young lady, that I put a roof over your head which is more than that feckless husband of yours did. I gave birth to you in that house and I did my best to give you a happy childhood. I saw to it that you wanted for nothing. How could you be could be so ungrateful? I can see I was right not to leave the house to you.*

Ruth ran to the sink and vomited violently.

★★★

"Where shall we go today, Beth? It's too cold for the park, what about the cinema?"

Ruth's gaze was not darting anxiously to the clock this morning. It was Sunday, no post came on Sundays. She loved Sundays. The thought of that one day of blessed escape was the only thing which dragged her through the misery of other six days of the week. She and Bethany could go out without any fear of what might be lying on the mat awaiting their return. She beamed eagerly at her daughter. She didn't care where they went. A trip to the local sewage farm would have seemed as glorious as a day in Paris, anywhere would be wonderful just as long they were out of that house.

Bethany's brown eyes darted round the kitchen. Ruth found herself glancing around too to see what was capturing the child's attention. A basket of clothes, awaiting ironing, overflowed in the corner. The dishes, though washed, still lay on the draining board. Last weeks' newspapers spilled over the edge of the table on their way to the recycle bin.

Bethany pulled a face. "I think we should stay in and tidy up, Mummy. Look it's filthy."

Ruth gaped at her daughter. "It's not. Just a few things needing to be put away, that's all. They can wait. Surely you'd rather go out for treat. I can tidy up next week when you're at school."

Bethany frowned. "But you didn't do it last week when I was at school, did you, Mummy? I hate things being untidy."

"What on earth has got into you —"

Bethany stamped her foot, like a toddler refused icecream. "I won't go out until it's tidy, Mummy, I won't! You can't make me!"

She ran from the room. Ruth, stunned by the outburst, heard her little feet stomping up the stairs.

"Bethany, come down this minute," she yelled up as a bedroom door slammed above her head.

The doorbell rang. Mrs Evans from next door was standing on the step, smiling and thrusting a white envelope into Ruth's hand.

"The postman put it through our letterbox by mistake yesterday. I meant to pop it round before, but we were so busy, you know how it is. Still I don't suppose it's important. It's from a child by the looks of the writing. Mind you, you don't often see children who've been taught neat handwriting nowadays, especially not in ink. I don't think my granddaughter's ever held a pen, it's all computers with her. Still, it's nice that some of the kids have still got the old fashioned values."

Ruth had to use every ounce of control she possessed to push her face muscles into the semblance of a polite smile.

She carried the letter into the sitting room and slammed it down on the table, burying her face in her hands. She wouldn't open it. She wouldn't, not today, not on the one day of the week she could escape from that evil, malicious old witch.

"Mummy?" Bethany appeared in the doorway.

Ruth tried to pull herself together and glanced up with a brittle smile. "What is it, angel?"

"You must remove the hyacinths from the airing cupboard now. The flowers won't form properly if you allow the leaves to grow on in the dark. The pots should have been taken out last week."

It was Bethany's voice, but wasn't the way Bethany spoke. It wasn't the way any six-year old child spoke.

"Beth? Where… where did you learn about hyacinths?"

Her daughter didn't answer. Instead she extended a single finger and ran it pointedly over the surface of the mahogany sideboard, leaving a thin shining line in the fine layer of dust. Her nose wrinkled in disapproval.

For a long moment, Ruth stared at that chubby finger. The nail was unbitten, and a white half-moon was already visible at the base, but that wasn't what held Ruth's attention. The skin of the small finger was stained with turquoise ink.

"Please attend to the hyacinths now," Bethany commanded sternly. "Don't leave them until it's too late as you usually do."

Ruth was aware that her head was throbbing. A sickly drowsiness swept over her. It was the smell; it was that overpowering sweet smell, so thick and heavy she could hardly breathe. She was choking on it, as if someone was holding a soft pillow over her face. She staggered towards the stairs, but she couldn't get away from it. She fell to her knees, clinging to the banister, gagging and gasping, but the smell was growing stronger with every passing tick of the clock. The stench of gardenia was seeping down and down, filling every room, oozing into every corner of the house. And Ruth knew this time it would not fade away.

Entreat me not to leave you, for whither I go, you shall go also.

Fondest love,
Mother

The Story About a Bus Driver Who Wanted to Be God

Etgar Keret

This is the story about a bus driver who would never open the door of the bus for people who were late. Not for anyone. Not for repressed highschool kids who'd run alongside the bus and stare at it longingly, and certainly not for highly strung people in windbreakers who'd bang on the door as if they were actually on time and it was the driver who was out of line, and not even for little old ladies with brown paper bags full of groceries who struggled to flag him down with trembling hands. And it wasn't because he was mean that he didn't open the door, because this driver didn't have a mean bone in his body; it was a matter of ideology. The driver's ideology said that if, say, the delay that was caused by opening the door for someone who came late was just under thirty seconds, and it not opening the door meant that this person would wind up losing fifteen minutes of his life, it would still he more fair to society to not open the door, because the thirty seconds would be lost by every single passenger on the bus. And if there were, say, sixty people on the bus who hadn't done anything wrong, and had all arrived at the bus stop on time, then together they'd be losing half an hour, which is double fifteen minutes. This was the only reason why he'd never open the door. He knew that the passengers hadn't the slightest idea what his reason was, and that the people running after the bus and signaling him to stop had no idea either. He also knew that most of them thought he was just a SOB, and that personally it would have been much much easier for him to let them on, and receive their smiles and thanks. Except that when it came to choosing between smiles and thanks, on the one hand, and the good of society, on the other, this driver knew what it had to be.

The person who should have suffered the most from the driver's ideology was named Eddie, but unlike the other people in this story, he wouldn't even try to run for the bus; that's how lazy and wasted he was. Now, Eddie was assistant cook at a restaurant called the Steakaway, which was the best pun that the stupid owner of the place could come up with. The food there was nothing to write home about, but Eddie himself was a really nice guy — so nice that sometimes, when something he made didn't come out too great, he'd serve it to the table himself and apologise. It was during one of these apologies that he met Happiness, or at least a shot at Happiness, in the form of a girl who was so sweet that she tried to finish the entire portion of roast beef that he brought her, just so he wouldn't feel bad. And this girl didn't want to tell him her name or give him her phone number, but she was sweet enough to agree to meet him the next day at five at a spot they decided on together — at the Dolphinarium, to be exact.

Now Eddie had this condition — one that had already caused him to miss out on all sorts of things in life. It wasn't one of those conditions where your adenoids get all swollen or anything like that, but still, it had already caused him a lot of damage. This sickness always made him oversleep by ten minutes, and no alarm clock did any good. That was why he was invariably late for work at the Steakaway — that and our

31

bus driver, the one who always chose the good of society over positive reinforcements on the individual level. Except that this time, since Happiness was at stake, Eddie decided to beat the condition, and instead of taking an afternoon nap he stayed awake and watched television. Just to be on the safe side, he even lined up not one but three alarm clocks and ordered a wake-up call to boot. But this sickness was incurable, and Eddie fell asleep like a baby, watching the kiddie channel. He woke up in a sweat to the screeching of a trillion million alarm clocks — ten minutes too late — rushed out of the house without stopping to change, and ran toward the bus stop. He barely remembered how to run anymore, and his feet fumbled a bit every time they left the sidewalk. The last time he ran was before he discovered that he could cut gym class, which was about in the sixth grade, except that unlike in those gym classes, this time he ran like crazy, because now he had something to lose, and all the pains in his chest and his Lucky Strike wheezing weren't going to get in the way of his pursuit of Happiness. Nothing was going to get in his way except our bus driver, who had just closed the door and was beginning to pull away. The driver saw Eddie in the rearview mirror, but as we've already explained, he had an ideology — a well reasoned ideology that, more than anything, relied on a love of justice and on simple arithmetic. Except that Eddie didn't care about the driver's arithmetic. For the first time in his life, he really wanted to get somewhere on time. And that's why he went right on chasing the bus, even though he didn't have a chance.

Suddenly, Eddie's luck turned, but only halfway: one hundred yards past the bus stop there was a traffic light. And, just a second before the bus reached it, the traffic light turned red. Eddie managed to catch up with the bus and drag himself all the way to the driver's door. He didn't even bang on the glass, he was so weak. He just looked at the driver with moist eyes and fell to his knees, panting and wheezing. And this reminded the driver of something — something from out of the past, from a time even before he wanted to become a bus driver, when he still wanted to become God. It was kind of a sad memory because the driver didn't become God in the end, but it was a happy one too, because he became a bus driver, which was his second choice. And suddenly the driver remembered how he'd once promised himself that if he became God in the end, He'd be merciful and kind and would listen to all His creatures. So when he saw Eddie from way up in his driver's seat, kneeling on the asphalt, he simply couldn't go through with it, and in spite of all his ideology and his simple arithmetic he opened the door, and Eddie got on — and didn't even say thank you, he was so out of breath.

The best thing would be to stop reading here, because even though Eddie did get to the Dolphinarium on time, Happiness couldn't come, because Happiness already had a boyfriend. It's just that she was so sweet that she couldn't bring herself to tell Eddie, so she preferred to stand him up. Eddie waited for her, on the bench they'd agreed on, for almost two hours. While he sat there he kept thinking all sorts of depressing thoughts about life, and while he was at it he watched the sunset, which was a pretty good one, and thought about how charley-horsed he was going to be later on. On his way back, when he was really desperate to get home, he saw his bus in the distance, pulling in at the bus stop and letting off passengers, and he knew that even if he'd had the strength to run, he'd never catch up with it anyway. So he just kept on walking slowly, feeling about a million tired muscles with every step, and when he finally reached the bus stop, he saw that the bus was still there, waiting for him. And even though the passengers were shouting and grumbling to get a move on, the driver waited for Eddie, and he didn't touch the accelerator till Eddie was seated. And when they started moving, he looked in the rearview mirror and gave Eddie a sad wink, which somehow made the whole thing almost bearable.

Translated by Mirium Shlesinger

Close
Jon McGregor

She wouldn't tell Patricia. She'd decided that before even saying goodbye, before she'd stood there and listened to his
footsteps crunch away through the gravel. What was there to
tell anyway. It was only talking.

And he'd approached her first. When they were standing in
the reception room, holding their information leaflets and
waiting for the tour of the Imperial Palace to begin. You're
English right, he'd said, and she'd nodded, and he'd asked if
they might swap cameras for the morning, for the duration of
the tour. Which she hadn't understood straight away. He
wanted his picture taken, he'd explained, with his camera, and
he wanted to return the favour. Which was no sort of favour
at all because she didn't like being in her own holiday photos. She knew what she looked like.

It'll save us swapping back and forth every time, he'd said.

It had seemed rude to say no, once he'd asked. And there
had been other people standing there, other people he could
have asked, but he'd asked her. Which was something.

He was in Japan for three weeks, he'd told her. Tokyo, Kyoto,
Osaka. The whole *shebang*. Spending his army pension,
because he figured 'what the hey it's just sitting there' and he
happened to have this time on his hands. He was *between jobs*,

he said, smiling in a way which was surprising for such a big man. Boyish was the word she thought of, although she didn't think he was any younger than her. Ex-US Army Engineers, so he'd seen a few countries in his time but had never been to Japan, always wanted to. Been working in a repair shop the last few years, welding, but the work had dried up. Living in Duluth, Minnesota, which when you figured all the countries he'd been through it was funny how it wasn't a million miles from where he'd started out. Good place to be, and it was handy for where his kids lived now.

He'd told her all this before the tour had even started, and in return she'd told him that she was a school secretary from Gainsborough, Lincolnshire, and that she was only here for a week. He'd done more of the talking, it was fair to say.

And when they'd introduced themselves, just as the tour began, he'd held out his hand for her to shake. Which she hadn't been expecting. He had a very large hand. He was really quite a large man, he looked sort of like a rugby player or something and she could see even from where she was standing that none of it was fat. Shaking hands with him, it had made her feel sort of petite. Which she certainly wasn't used to.

Wade, he'd said. Elizabeth, she'd replied.

That room though. If they were going to have that many people waiting in there for the tours to begin, they should have had a fan or something. Air conditioning. It was too hot, really. Close.

He'd asked her to take the first picture almost immediately, as the group was walking across the great expanse of white sun-blasted gravel, the crunch of their footsteps swallowed up by the hot still air. Framing himself against the first of the Palace buildings while she lifted his camera to her face.

And if she does tell someone about this when she gets home, not Patricia but someone at least, then she'll say that this was when she first noticed, properly, what he looked like. There was the moustache, of course, and the sheer solid size of the man. But there was something else, something soft and quiet in his face and his eyes, something that contrasted with his loud talk and his oversized hands. It was nice, looking at him like that through the viewfinder.

They'd changed places then, as the rest of the group moved further away, and she'd felt her already flushed face colour further as he'd looked at her through her camera, and wished she'd been wearing a different outfit. Something cooler. Something less pink. And something other than that pair of trousers. Patricia had told her before that they didn't work — they don't do anything to help with your size is all I'm saying, she'd said, the only time Elizabeth had worn them in the office — but she'd got up in a hurry that morning and they were the first thing that had come to hand, and the whole outfit had looked nice in the air-conditioned hotel room, had looked cool and elegant and English roseish. But now, standing for a picture she didn't want taken anyway, she just felt hot, and pink, and fat. And so why did she even think he might have been interested. She wasn't seventeen anymore. Not by a long way.

The tour guide had already started by the time they'd caught up with the rest of the group. His Imperial Majesty would arrive from long journey in ox-drawn carriage, she was saying, pronouncing *ox-der-awn-car-riage* very precisely, as if it was essential that they understood. She described the entrance building behind her, with its low flight of steps and receding series of empty, cavernous rooms lined with painted silk screens and tatami mat floors.

She'd felt Wade nudging her. How d'you find life in Gainsborrow? he'd whispered. She'd been a bit embarrassed that he was talking while the guide was talking, but still.

It's Gains*borough*, she'd whispered back, and he'd put his hand over his mouth and made an apologetic face, which was nice that he thought it was important. Sorry, he'd whispered; how's life in *Gains-bor-ough*, splitting the word up the way the tour guide had done with ox-drawn carriage, which was maybe a bit mean but very funny as well the way he did it, and so then it had been her turn to put her hand over her mouth, to hide her laughter.

They'd clicked very quickly, that was the thing. That was something else that was new.

So, the guide had said then; please now to the *Oi-ke-ni-wa* Garden. And everyone had turned and followed her across the gravel, except that by some silent agreement Wade and Elizabeth had waited and lagged a short way behind.

Wade and Elizabeth. It had a ring to it, but what was she thinking.

She'd asked him if he liked living in Minnesota, and he'd said sure it was fine, it was home, and he'd mentioned again that it was good to be near to his kids. He'd asked her if she enjoyed being a school secretary, and she'd said she supposed there were worse jobs she could be doing. He'd laughed, and said that was true enough, and she'd asked about his children, she'd said you said your children are nearby, are they at university or something? Surprising herself even as she said it, because she didn't always find small talk easy but this time she had. Which had made her think.

He'd looked at her, and she'd realised straight away that she'd missed the point, and he'd said no they're too young for that just yet. They're living with their mother.

Oh, she'd said. I'm sorry. I didn't think.

No, it's okay, he'd said. It was a while ago now. These things happen, you know how it is. He'd made a face, a sort of knowing frown, as if to say I'd rather not go into details but I'm sure you can guess. She wasn't sure that she could. You got children? he asked.

No, she said, no I haven't.

He looked like he was waiting for her to add something, but she didn't. Because what would she have said. Because what else was there to say.

The other people on the tour had all been younger than her and Wade, and she'd wondered how it was that young people these days seemed able to travel anywhere in the world that took their fancy. This was just one holiday among many for them, and the ones who didn't know each other already were asking about it; none of them saying *where are you from*, she noticed, but rather *where've you been* and *where you headed?* One of them, a tall American girl in a sleeveless top and a pair of sensible walking shorts, all long brown limbs and neat blonde hair, had turned to Wade and said *hey how's it going*, as the tour guide led them through the garden to the next talking point, and Wade had said *hey good thanks* in reply. Leaving Elizabeth sort of a bit stranded as they started a conversation of their own.

It was a beautiful garden. There was a lake, a large pond really, with a low arched bridge at one end, and a pebbled shore, and a stream winding down towards it from a stand of bamboo. There were the usual clipped and twisted trees, and carefully arranged rocks, and mossy seating areas. The whole garden felt natural and artificial at the same time, and she wondered if there were hidden meanings to the arrangement which you were meant to decode. She'd wanted to say something to Wade about it, but he'd still been talking.

That girl though. It must be sunny all the time where she was from, going by how tanned those long slim limbs were, the carefree freckles on her face. She must have never lost a night's sleep over anything, she'd thought, and been surprised by her own bitterness. Because was this who she'd become, already. She tried to remember, and she couldn't, when she'd last been able to wear shorts, or anything without sleeves.

What sort of a name was *Wade* anyway, she'd found herself thinking.

So, please, the guide had said then; please, this is *Oh-ga-ku-mon-jo*. In festival times poetry recitals would be held here, she'd said, and gestured towards a painted silk screen in an open room beside the garden. The painting showed a group of finely dressed courtiers sitting cross-legged in a garden, and the guide had explained that the painting was of the garden behind them. If you look they are sitting beside stream, she'd said; and this is same stream here, with same group of three rocks also.

She just didn't know her way around this sort of thing, was the problem. She wasn't familiar with the territory. She couldn't read the situation, if there was ever a situation to read. Patricia had told her once that she was better off without a man, that she couldn't imagine the trouble they caused. Elizabeth assumed she'd meant well, but she really hadn't appreciated it. She'd said Patricia if I want your opinion on my private life I'll ask and until then I'd rather not have that sort of comment thank you. Which Patricia hadn't responded to, but when she'd refilled the paper tray on the photocopier she'd slammed it so hard that Elizabeth had been surprised it didn't break.

At these poetry recitals there was a particular tradition, the guide had continued, gesturing towards the painted screen again; there would be small cups of sake in folded paper boats floating down from the top of the stream. And aim was to invent short poem on given subject before boat reaches you, she said; if you could not think of poem quickly enough then you were not permitted to drink sake, you must allow boat to pass by.

Which would be enough to make you never want to go to a garden party again, she'd thought. Being put on the spot like that. Watching the little paper boat wobble past you and not being able to think of a thing to say. Because it would feel sort of exposed, something like that.

The tour guide had smiled then, and asked if there were any questions, and led the group off towards the last point of the tour. Elizabeth had hung back for a moment, looking at the painted screen, the four figures seated on the moss around the stream. They were so plump it was difficult to see if they were men or women, their long black hair coiled around their heads, their kimonos folded richly around them. They didn't look nervous. They didn't look as if they'd have trouble thinking of something witty and poetic in the short time they had, reciting their lines, reaching out to take the cup before the paper boat had passed them, before it folded and crumpled into the water and the sake spilt away downstream.

Wade had been waiting for her at the exit, smiling. I was starting to worry about you, he said. To which, she hadn't known how to reply. And then he'd said so, I guess that's us, isn't it?

Yes, she said. I suppose it is.

He'd lowered his head to take her camera off from round his neck, and for a moment she'd thought he was bowing in the traditional Japanese style, and she'd started to bow in return before she'd realised he wasn't at all. And she was sure he'd noticed, but he didn't say anything. Which stuck in her mind, because some people would have laughed at her right there. But he didn't laugh. He shook her hand again, and said goodbye, and see you then, and take care.

And she decided, as she stood in the deep green shade of a cypress tree and listened to his footsteps crunch away along the gravelled path, to go back and have another look at the Palace garden. She wanted to get a picture of the stream, and the rocks, and the small stand of bamboo trees. If she was quick she could get back in before the Palace guides closed up, before they swung the gates closed and put out the No Entry signs and asked her to come back and try again another day.

Flies
Eshkol Nevo

It was the last summer before they gave the Sinai back to Egypt. I was thirteen and I drove with my parents and their friends down to Ras Burka. I think that must have been our last big family trip. After that, I preferred going with my friends. In any case, one of the families traveling with us had a son with cerebral palsy. They put up their tent a little bit away from the rest of us so it took a few days before I even noticed him. And that was purely by accident too. I went into the water to snorkel and the current carried me too far out. The waves were high, salt water seeped into my snorkel and my mask steamed up. I wanted to go back to the shore but didn't know how. After a long moment, I found a sandy path that wound through the corals and swam along it till I reached the shore. I rested there for a while, got my breathing regular again, took off my fins and started walking back toward our tent, swearing to myself that this was the last time I'd go underwater by myself.

And then I saw him.

He was sitting in a wheelchair near his family's tent.

I couldn't decide whether to go over to him, but he seemed to be smiling at me, so I turned away from the shoreline and walked toward him. When I got closer, I saw that the smile was actually an involuntary twitch that distorted his mouth.

But that wasn't the main thing.

Dozens of flies were sitting on his face. There were flies on his lips, on his nose, inside his nose, in his ears, on his cheeks, his neck, his chin, his hair, his weird thick glasses. Big flies, small flies, flies that weren't moving, flies that were rubbing their hands together in pleasure. Where were his parents? How could they have left him there like that?

"Do something," his eyes pleaded from behind his glasses. "Save me from this torture." He moaned, the sound an animal makes. A wounded animal.

I peeled off my shirt and started flapping it wildly around his body. Some of the flies took off. And some didn't. I waved my other hand too, and kicked the air with my foot, close to his face. I did everything but touch him. I jumped and stamped, even went into their tent and brought out a piece of cardboard meant for fanning the barbecue coals, and waved it hard next to the back of his neck where an especially stubborn guerilla of a fly was hanging on.

Finally, after a few minutes of hard work, I managed to cut down the number of flies by half. I knew that as soon as I left him, the flies would come back and retake his face easily. But there was no choice. I had to go back to the main tent for help.

"I'll be right back," I said. He didn't nod his head and he didn't shake it. I thought I could see a thank you in his eyes, but I wasn't sure of that either. "I'll be right back," I repeated. And again, not a muscle in his face moved.

I started running back to the main tent, the soles of my feet burning in the sand, but before I reached it, I ran into his parents, who must have been on their way back. The mother was carrying their new, blond baby girl. The father was carrying two folding chairs.

Your son, I blurted out, he's there... alone... the flies. The words were all jumbled in my mouth.

We know, the father said in a firm voice. Confident. What can we do, the mother said with a sigh. We can't stand next to him all day and swat them away.

Yes, but... I wanted to object. To demand. To wave my fins around. But my protest couldn't find its way into words, into a coherent argument. I was only thirteen and still a little bit afraid of grownups.

But thanks for taking an interest, the father said, and started walking again. She has sensitive skin, it isn't good for her, being in the sun like this, the mother apologised, gesturing to the little blond girl, and walked past me. The little blond girl herself was asleep, her face bright and beautiful.

That night, I told my parents about it. I was sure they'd be outraged. That they'd use the same expressions they used when I did something to make them furious: "shameful," "disgraceful," or worst of all — "deplorable."

To my shock, they were indifferent. Even worse: it turned out that it was nothing new for them. The boy had been with the group on their vacation at Lake Kinneret, and then too, he sat in his wheelchair outside the tent and the flies set up residence on him.

I agree with you, it's not a pretty sight, my father said. But what can they do? Stand next to him all day and swat away the flies?

I actually think it's nice that they insist on bringing him, my mother added. After all, they could leave him in the home. But they want him to grow up like a normal child.

So why do they hide him? the question burst out of me at full volume, volume that was fine for home, not the Sinai. If it's so nice and they have nothing to be ashamed of, why did they put up their tent so far from everyone else?!

Because it took them a little more time to get organised

and that was the only place left for them, my father said.

Yes, my mother backed him up — I hadn't heard her back him up on anything for a long time — it's purely by chance. At the Kinneret, they were right in the centre of things.

Their arguments, added on to his parents' arguments, paralyzed me. It all sounded so logical and convincing. But still, I had the feeling that an injustice was being done here. My father put out the candle and in the dark, my mother said it was nice that I thought about others, not only about myself, and maybe I should put that virtue to use by washing the plastic plates every once in a while because it makes no sense that she's in the Sinai and the only thing she does all day is cook and wash up after us.

When we woke up the next morning, we saw that a lot of other Israeli families had come during the night and planted their tents on the beach. You can't imagine, Rina, the whole country came to say goodbye to the Sinai, my father said after finishing his morning exercises outside the tent. Oh my God, my mother said when she went outside, the whole country really is here.

I hated it when they talked like that. As if they weren't actually part of the country. But I didn't say anything. I went outside and scanned the beach. The boy's tent wasn't on the edge of the camp anymore, but right in the middle of the rows of tents that now filled the small inlet from the little hill to the dunes. Terrific, I said to myself, now the whole country will see that boy being tortured on his wheelchair and someone will definitely say something to his parents.

That day, when the sun had begun to sink toward the hills, I went into the water with my snorkel and swam back to the spot where the narrow sandy path wound between the large fire corals. After I came out of the water and dried myself off on the beach, I began looking for their tent. It wasn't easy to find anymore because there were so many other tents surrounding it, but the flash of the sun's rays on the iron of the wheelchair showed me the way.

He was sitting there in the same small square of shade. I searched his eyes for a sign that he recognised me, remembered something. And didn't find it. There were a million flies on his face. A billion. The whole country has been walking past him since the morning, I thought. And didn't do a thing.

I started the work of swatting them away. This time, I was determined to get all the flies, every last one. I wanted to see his face completely clear for once, I wanted to give him a few seconds grace, free of irritation.

It took a long time — the sun was already turning the hilltops golden — but in the end, I did it. The last three flies turned out to be dead, and I peeled them off his cheek with my fingers. But while I was moving back a little to check if any flies had gotten away from me, four new ones landed on his nose.

Furious, I went back and slapped the air next to his nose until they gave up and flew away. Then I stood beside him for a few minutes to make sure that not a single fly dared to come back. It was starting to get dark and I hoped my parents were already worrying about me, so I promised the fly boy that I'd come back the next day at the same time, and left.

I'd like to say that I went back the next day and the day after that. I'd like to say that, in the end, I started a protest demonstration, maybe even a hunger strike, near the fly boy's wheelchair until his parents had no choice but to stand on either side of him waving huge palm fronds all day long.

But at the moment, the truth is stronger than me.

That evening, near one of the circles of people listening to a guitar player, I met a fifteen-year-old girl. I lied to her, said I was fifteen too, and she believed me and told me that in

Ashdod, where she lived, there are some girls who'd gone all the way with older boys. She had big green eyes and chocolate skin, and she always wore a white bikini, day and night, and spoke loudly about her boobs, how big and beautiful they were. I fell in love with her instantly, of course. And I spent the next few days playing endless games of backgammon with her and her cousins, trying desperately to impress her.

One afternoon, her cousins went into the water and just the two of us were left on the beach. The sun was behind us. I didn't turn around, but I could picture it turning the hill-tops golden now.

We didn't talk. I felt that it was my responsibility to rescue us from the silence.

There's this kid here, I said. He has some disease, I don't what. Anyway, his parents leave him in a wheelchair outside their tent the whole day, and all the flies in the Sinai come and sit on his face.

How disgusting, she said.

Yes, I agreed. And added, spitting out the words quickly, I go to see him every once in a while and swat away the flies. Want to come with me?

What, now? she asked and buried her tan legs in the soft sand like someone who has no intention of going anywhere.

No, I said, alarmed. Who said now? I was thinking later, tomorrow.

We'll see, maybe, she said, and jumped up suddenly. You coming in the water?

I didn't see the boy with the flies anymore. I was sure I'd see him the last day when my parents' whole gang took down their tents and gathered together to make the trip to Eilat in a convoy of Subarus. I planned to tell his parents a thing or two, or at least say goodbye to him and apologise for not

48

keeping my promise, but when we got to the meeting place, his family wasn't there.

They left yesterday, my mother explained. Their little girl had a bad upset stomach.

And what about the… I started to ask, but my father changed the subject. Son, he said, take one last look at the beach and make sure you remember what you see. Inside of a year, the Egyptians will build an army base here. And that's the end of the corals and the fish.

No, my mother said, I think they'll develop the place for tourism.

And he answered her.

And she answered him.

And they were off, arguing till Eilat, and maybe even till we were on the Arava Road, I don't know, because after Kibbutz Yotvata, I fell asleep.

A few months later, the Sinai went back to Egypt and became cleaner and quieter.

Ras Burka was taken over by an unpleasant blue-eyed Egyptian sheikh and his German wife. They let Israelis in the first few years, but then the intifada started and they hung out a little cardboard sign saying that only people with European passports could enter.

The pretty girl from Ashdod starred in my fantasies for a few months. And when I couldn't summon up her face anymore, I replaced her with Sharon Haziz, the latest, hottest singer.

I haven't thought about the boy with the flies for years, but during my last stint in the reserves — I was posted in Nablus, and when it was over, I asked for a transfer to a different unit — I suddenly remembered him. I was sitting alone in the small shed at the Ein Huwara checkpoint counting stars, listening to fragmented conversations on the radio, and I don't really know why, but that boy's face floated up before my eyes and my heart swelled all at once to the size of a watermelon, good God, there were even flies on his eyelashes, in his nostrils, in his ears. And I'd promised him I'd come.

A thought buzzed in my mind: it's funny that I never mention the incident to anyone. After all, I've revealed more embarrassing things to the world — secrets, lies, perversions — but for some reason, not that. I promised myself I'd tell my wife when I got home, I felt that I had to tell at least her, but when I got home, the twins had fever and we took turns sitting with them and hardly had any time to talk.

Later I forgot about it. And I have no idea why I remembered it now, of all times. That terrible reserve duty was a year and a half ago, and I'm sitting at the computer now to prepare a laser optics marketing presentation for tomorrow morning. All the company's head honchos will be there, and I still have a lot of work, so many slides that aren't ready yet, so many slides I have to proof-read, and obviously, this is a text I won't show anyone. Obviously, it'll be buried in the depths of my hard disk, where it'll keep buzzing.

Translated by Sondra Silverston

Stealing Memories
Richard Zimler

In September of 1931, the French painter Fernand Léger visited the United States for the first time. He was fifty years old
and already famous for his darkly outlined, colourful figures.
In early October, while in New York, one of his lower molars
became infected. At the time, my father did all the dental
work for Marcel Berenger, the Madison Avenue gallery
owner. One evening, Berenger called our home. Could his
close friend and compatriot Léger come by that night?

Near midnight, Léger arrived wearing a tweed coat and
cap. My father told me years later, "He had panicked eyes, and
I knew he was going to be a difficult patient." In fact, he sat
frozen in the dental chair and mumbled in French when my
father didn't have his hands in his mouth. Was he cursing?
Praying? My father spoke little French and couldn't say for
sure.

"I remember that he sweated a lot and that he smelled of
some peculiar floral soap," Dad told me.

The problematic molar was easily cleaned and filled. Léger
shook my father's hands exuberantly and thanked him with
great praise for his dental skills. In his awkward English, he
confessed that the toothache had made him forgetful, and that
he only had two American one dollar bills in his wallet — just
enough for cab fare back to his hotel. Of course, he had no

checking account in America. If my father were willing to wait until the next day, he would mail a cheque drawn on Monsieur Berenger's account. My father said not to bother, that it was his pleasure to work on the molar of so talented an artist. Léger reluctantly agreed and parted a happy man.

Exactly three days later, however, a small flat package arrived by messenger. It was twelve inches square, wrapped with brown paper and tied with red and white bakery string. "I thought your Aunt Rutya had sent us some of her strange Rumanian pastry," my father told me with a laugh. Inside the package, however, was a small painting Léger had apparently just completed and a signed, two-word note written in French: *Avec gratitude.*

As children, my brother, two sisters and I called the painting, "The Woman with Stone Hair."

It's a portrait of a young woman seated on the ground with long black tresses done in such a way as to make them look solid — like polished obsidian. She has the soft pink skin and dreamy face typical of Léger's female portraits at the time.

The painting was my introduction to modern art. It used to hang in my parents' room, above their bed. Years later, I realised that it must have been a study for Léger's famous work, "The Bather," completed in 1932.

Both my parents adored the painting, and after my mother's death, it seemed to take on the importance of an icon for my father. Sometimes, I'd find him sitting on the green armchair where he usually piled his dirty clothing, holding the canvas, daydreaming. Once, late at night, I found him asleep with the Léger on his lap. At the time, I had no idea why. Children sometimes don't understand the simplest things.

My mother died on June 6, 1954, of breast cancer. By the time the lump was detected by our family doctor, the disease had spread to her lymph nodes. I was thirteen at the time. I didn't understand why her hair was falling out. My dad explained that Mom was really sick but that I shouldn't worry about her; she was getting the best possible care.

Before I realised that she was dying, she was already dead.

My mother and I had been very close. During her illness, we played endless games of gin rummy after school. Sometimes she liked to draw portraits of me. I'd sit in her bedroom by the windows facing Gramercy Park where the light was strong. She'd sit on her bed with her box of coloured pencils. She wore a bright blue beanie to keep her bald head warm. Her eyes were large and brown. She smiled a lot, as if to encourage me. As she sketched, she nibbled bits of Hershey's chocolate bars; it was the only food she could keep down.

Sometimes, she and I would clear off the dining room table and paint together with the sets of Japanese ink that my father found for us at a tiny art supply store on Hudson Street. Mostly she'd paint finches nesting in pine trees. I have two of these studies hanging in my office at Barnard College. Visitors always say, "Oh, so you've been to Japan..."

One strange little painting that she did hangs in my bedroom, however, over my bed. It's a finch, but it has human eyes — *my* eyes.

My mother was buried at Mt. Sinai Cemetery in Roslyn, out on Long Island. I refused to go to the ceremony and spent the afternoon alone, eating the rest of her chocolate bars in front of the television until I got sick and threw up all over an old Persian rug we had at the time.

After she died, I felt as if I'd been left behind on a cold and deserted planet. It was my father who rescued me. He let me come into his bed at night for a couple months after her death, never uttered even a single complaint for my disturbing his sleep. Nor did he listen to my older siblings' warnings that a 51-year-old man shouldn't share the same bed as his adolescent son. "Forget what they say," he used to tell me. "They don't understand." To get me to stop shivering and fall asleep, he'd rub my hair gently and tell me stories of his youth back in Poland. He spoke of demons from Gehenna, *shtetls* turned magically upside down, chickens with angels in their eggs. He took great pains to make all the endings happy.

On my insistence, he wrote down two of these stories and tried sending them to children's publishers, but all we got back were mimeographed rejection letters. Editors didn't regard *dybbuks* and Cossacks as fitting for American children. I still have the manuscripts at the bottom of my linen closet; maybe Jewish lore will come into fashion one day.

My brother and sisters were off on their own by the time my mother died; they were all in their twenties and married. So for the next six years, till I went off to college, my father and I lived alone in our apartment at the corner of Irving Place and East 20th Street. He was a good man, heartbreakingly lonely and prone to distant silences, but attentive when I needed him. After my mother's death, the pride which she'd taken in my smallest accomplishments was magically transferred to him, just like in one of his crazy stories. When I won my high school English award, he sat in the front row of the parent assembly with the tears of an immigrant father streaming down his cheeks.

When my father turned sixty-five, he sold his dental practice and moved permanently into a cottage in Hampton Bays out on Long Island. He gardened, watched New York Met's baseball games, and scratched out Bach suites on his violin. I spent every other weekend with him.

In later years, when New York winters forced him indoors for weeks at a time, he spent all of January and February with me at my apartment on 91st Street and West End Avenue. He'd read his magic realist novels in the bed that I set up in my living room, snooze, water my plants, browse in the local bookstores. When I'd get home from classes, he'd make me verbena tea. I used to make him jambalaya, his favourite dish, every Saturday.

In February of 1984, he suffered a minor stroke. In the hospital, he developed bacterial pneumonia. Then, something seemed to snap inside him and he grew delirious. One specialist said Alzheimer's disease. A couple others suggested various pathogens that could cause brain lesions. Tests were ordered, but none proved conclusive. It was agreed by default that Alzheimer's had set in, that he'd managed to keep it hidden until illness weakened him. He was 81 years old. I was the only child still living in New York. That spring, I took a leave of absence from my post in the Art History Department at Barnard and spent long afternoons in his cottage, keeping things clean, preparing meals, reading to him on occasion, and watching him snooze. He grew progressively weaker and would sleep most of the time, in the most cockeyed positions, legs and arms dangling over the side of his bed, his head twisted to the side and mouth open. One day, I dared to straighten him out and discovered that he was pliable, like a rag doll. I gingerly moved his legs together and placed his head straight back into the valley of his down pillow. He looked as if he were prepared for burial. So I took his right arm and laid it over the side of the bed and twisted his head. He looked much better that way.

Anyway, the important thing is that after I arranged my father in his bed, I noticed out his window that the crabapple tree in the backyard had become a cloud of soft pink. And that a male cardinal had alighted there. Red feathers and pink petals — life doesn't get much better than that.

Now, a decade later, I still associate the cardinal and the crabapple with my father's illness. When he wasn't sleeping, he'd sometimes kick and scream, froth at the mouth, rant about being held hostage. Toward the end, during the few moments of lucidity that gave both of us a bit of peace, he'd reach for me. "Paulie, you're still here," he'd say. "When will it end?"

His grip was that of an eagle; talons biting into flesh.

Then he would begin to shout again. "I want out! Out! You can't keep me here against my will. I want to see the manager! Where's the manager?"

Pieces of the verbal puzzle I put together made it clear that he often thought he was being held captive in a hotel in San Francisco. At other times, he was convinced he was being dunked underwater by a Cossack marauder — and that his entire village of Jews was being butchered.

I found out that an eighty-one-year-old fights like a teenaged boxer to keep from drowning. His doctor recommended low dosages of tranquilisers. Half a five-milligram Valium usually did the trick.

Once, during a calm moment, I found him sitting on his bed facing the Léger, just like in the old days. We held hands without talking, and then he struggled to his feet to make us verbena tea as a treat.

All of us who loved my father knew he had been constructed of more fragile materials than most people — a man of balsa wood with a rubber-band engine flying off to foreign lands inside his head. So dementia was not totally unexpected. In fact, my two sisters and brother all told me — independently of one another — that they were only surprised he'd stayed sane for so long. They said it easily, as if they were discussing a family pet who'd been gently weakened by an invisible cancer.

My own interpretation of the visions my father had that spring is that there was always a kind of fairytale landscape inside him that engulfed him completely in the end. It was a world of *shtetls* hidden deep inside the forests of Poland — a land of Talmud scholars and kabbalistic magic, but also one of Cossacks and pogroms.

For many years, he escaped such a world successfully, but then, when he weakened physically, it claimed him back.

As we reach the end of our lives, do we all return to our ancestral landscape? Will I, too, return to the threatening forests of Poland even though I've never set foot inside that country?

After he died, when I was sitting alone by his side, listening to the room exhale with relief, I began to tremble. There was no one there to make me verbena tea or rub my hair. No cardinal perched in the crabapple tree.

For about a week, I didn't feel anything but the gaping absence left by his death. My brother and sisters flew in for the funeral. They were willing to help by then because there was no one to nurse. They brought me barbecue chicken from the deli in Hampton Bays and cookies to nibble on in bed. Sometimes I'd go to Westhampton Beach, where I could walk down the strand and think about the past.

I didn't go to the funeral itself; that morning, my body seemed to give out, and I woke up shivering with a high fever and stomach cramps. I wasn't sorry; I was dreading having to share my grief with people who didn't help me take care of him.

Like my mom, the only thing I could keep down was chocolate. Real food tasted thick and stale.

Two weeks after my father died, I was alone in his house, beginning to inventory the Florida seashells, ceramic figurines, glass paperweights, and other *tsatskes* that he and my mother had accumulated over the years. It was then that I discovered that the painting by Léger was missing. "The Woman with Stone Hair" had been in his bedroom, of course, right above his nest of pillows. I'd seen it there every day for three months while nursing him. All that was left of it was a tawny square where the sun hadn't been able to bleach the wall.

I didn't panic. I called up my brother and two sisters to see if they'd seen it; they were the only people who'd spent any more than a few minutes at my father's house since his death.

I called each of them in turn, and they all denied knowing anything about the painting's disappearance.

I don't believe that my describing the personalities of my siblings will help anyone understand why they lied to me. What is important to know is that they hated my father for things that had happened many years before I came along, during their childhoods. After his death, they each made a point of telling me that he was a very different person when they were growing up: strict, unfeeling, vindictive. He didn't listen to them or our mother. They said he liked to humiliate the kids by slapping them in the face when they misbehaved.

They all mentioned these things to explain why they weren't visibly upset at his death. They spoke forcefully and slowly, as if they were prosecutors presenting the evidence against him.

Although it's hard for me to believe, I suppose that their portrait of my father may be accurate; after all, children grow up in different families according to their age. Also, parents often grow more tolerant as their youthful self-righteousness fades, and very possibly my father had changed his whole attitude toward childrearing by the time I came along. Another possibility is that his relationship with my mother improved over the years; when I knew them, my parents were affectionate and playful with each other. Apparently, that was not always the case.

When I told my older brother Mark about the painting, he raised his eyebrows in a theatrical way. "I didn't even know Dad still had it," he said matter-of-factly.

Hard to believe he could forget a painting worth a few hundred thousand dollars, but I didn't say anything.

When I called Sarah, next in line in our hierarchy, she shouted: "You lost it? You lost the Léger?"

I replied, "It was right there all the time. And then it was gone. Someone stole it."

"How could they steal it?" she moaned. "You were living in the house."

"I wasn't watching every minute. Someone could have walked in, just picked it off the wall and carried it off. If you'll remember, I was pretty depressed at the time and wasn't thinking about such things."

"Well you should have been thinking about them, because now you've really screwed things up. You should have put it in a vault, goddammit."

Then I called Florence, number three in our line of descent. When I was a kid, I was close to her. She played baseball with me, took me to foreign films, taught me how to roller skate in Gramercy Park. She had been bright and daring, had had thick dark hair, a quick smile, and long, elegant hands. After my mother died, however, she hardly ever came to visit me and my father. Now, she considered herself the only intelligent member of our family — the scholar. She taught Anthropology at Oberlin College and spent her summers digging up Hittite tablets in Turkey. She had neither a lover nor partner — no children, no friends. Her conversations with me had grown more and more bitter over the years. She was like a neverending winter whose days grow darker and colder with each coming year. Her particular brand of contempt for our father had mostly to do with him supposedly belittling her for pursuing an academic career. She hated me because I didn't hate him.

"That's just great," she told me when I informed her about the missing Léger. "Do you know how much money I make a year?"

"More than me, probably."

"Clever," she said. I could see her sneering. "I need that money," she continued. "We could've auctioned it and made a fortune. I was counting on it."

"So what do you want me to say?"

"You could start with you're sorry."

I let an angry silence spread between us to let her know that she'd reached the limits of my patience. She understood, and she spoke more gently. "Did they leave any clues?" she asked.

"None that I could find."

"So who could it be?"

"The only people who ever entered Dad's bedroom were me, you, Sarah and Mark."

She suddenly shouted, "If you're making this up... if you've hidden it so you can sell it later, I'll kill you!"

"Florence, what the hell are you..."

She was screeching at the top of her lungs: "I swear I'll kill you, I'll cut out your heart, and I won't give it another thought."

That was the first time I thought that something might be seriously wrong with her.

The police came twice to my father's cottage to dust for fingerprints and interview me. Florence even insisted on hiring a private detective. We each chipped in seven hundred and fifty dollars. But the painting didn't turn up. Until three weeks ago.

Meanwhile, within months of the painting disappearing, we all stopped talking to each other. At first, Florence suspected me, Sarah suspected Mark, and Mark suspected Florence. It was like a bad imitation of Shakespearean comedy. Then things got really wild; Florence convinced the others that the villain could only have been me. After all, I was the only one who'd been at my father's cottage all the time. So I had far more opportunity to take the painting and find a buyer. As for my motive, that was harder for her to concoct, since I'd never been known to care that much about any inheritance. But she managed to come up with one. According to Florence, I needed the money to pay secret debts. Her diabolical reasoning went as follows:

I'd been promiscuous during the 1970s and had therefore caught AIDS. I'd stolen the painting because I didn't want to admit that I had the disease and desperately needed to make hospital payments. Of course, I could have used my Barnard medical coverage, but I didn't want to confess my illness to university administrators for fear of being ostracised, even fired. This was 1984, and that sort of cramped reasoning made some sense back then. Anyway, Florence claimed that she'd actually searched through my garbage and found bills for thousands of dollars that had been stamped overdue by Roosevelt Hospital. Naturally, she said, I couldn't admit that I'd stolen the painting or had such hospital bills because to admit either would be to virtually confess that I was tainted with plague.

I found all this out from Sarah's eldest daughter, Rachel, the only person in the family with the courage to call me up and ask if I was really ill.

Thanks to Florence's creative storytelling, my three siblings have never talked to me again.

It has always been hard for me to believe that reasonably intelligent and sensitive adults could behave like this, especially if they really thought that I had AIDS. But, as I found out, such things happen all the time. Since the end of 1984, I've never even received so much as a Christmas card or birthday call from any of them. And until three weeks ago, I really did believe that they accepted Florence's story. I figured that they must have regarded it as an absolute miracle that I managed to live more than a few years.

During kind moments, I used to say to myself that when Florence started these rumours everybody was in a panic about the new plague striking America. And my father had just died. None of us was behaving rationally.

Occasionally, however, I speculated that Florence had stolen the painting and had accused me to cover herself. But mostly, I didn't care. Dad was dead. I had a tenured teaching job that kept me fulfilled, good health and close friends. At a time when people really were starting to die in the long, drawn-out viral war that was just then beginning, these were the important things. As for the painting, I hoped that it had been sold to a museum where people could appreciate the nobility of the peasant girl with the obsidian hair. If I gave in to anger at times, it was only because I thought that the loss of the painting had somehow ripped out the very last page of my father's life story.

Then, one June day in 2001, I flew off to Porto, Portugal to attend a series of lectures on French 20th-Century Figurative Painting at the Serralves Foundation, expecting not much more than seeing a few old friends. Martin Roland was there, the painter and professor of Art History at McGill University. The title of his talk was "Léger, the Female Nude and Solitude." I didn't know what this meant exactly, but I liked the way it sounded. During his lecture, he showed slides to illustrate his theory that Léger's women were fundamentally more isolated than his men — that they inhabited what he called *espaces fermées* — closed spaces. Additionally, Roland suggested that such an attitude was fundamentally new; the Classic and Romantic attitude being that women were far more in touch with the world — connected to the cycles of birth and death — than men. One of the slides illustrating Roland's thesis was of my father's painting.

When I saw it, I gasped; it was as if a loved one had risen from the grave. *So is she still here?* I thought; I realised at that moment that I'd imagined for many years that the young woman in the painting had died at the same moment as my father. Strange what the mind comes up with.

More importantly, I also realised that the young woman in the painting looked like my mother. How I could have missed that is beyond me. Maybe it was the trauma of losing her. Or maybe I needed to be older to see the subtle correspondence in their attitude rather than their physical form. There was no denying, however, that they had the same serene but knowing look in their eyes, the same inner elegance. Was this a coincidence? Or had Léger met my mother that night when he came to have his molar filled? Maybe he, too, recognised the similarity and offered the painting in tribute.

When Martin's lecture ended, I ran to him to ask about "The Woman with Stone Hair."

"I got the slide from the Fondation Maeght," he replied. "I suppose the painting must be there, but I've never actually seen it in person."

From my hotel I called up the Fondation Maeght in Nice and spoke to a helpful young woman who told me that the painting in question was owned by a private collector in Princeton, New Jersey. She was a miracle worker and called me back later the same day with his phone number and name — Carlo Ricci.

When I spoke to Mr. Ricci from Portugal, he was friendly. Yes, he had the painting. It was hanging in his living room, over his couch. He remembered very well the circumstances under which he'd bought it. He voice was deep, his accent slightly British.

"At the time, I was collecting Léger, everything I could find," he told me. "I was in love with his scope, his size. A dealer in Boston called me one day. Jensen... Richard Lloyd Jensen. Do you know him?"

"I'm afraid not."

"Well, he called me up one day, out of the blue, and he said he had a lovely portrait in the style of 'The Bather,' and that the people who owned it wanted to get rid of it quickly — that I could get it for a bargain price."

"Did he say who it was who was selling it?"

"Not that I recall."

"You wouldn't have Mr. Jensen's number, by any chance?"

"I have his gallery number. If you'll wait just a moment..."

But Ricci couldn't turn up the number; he'd stopped buying paintings years before and had moved on to antique cars.

When I got home a few days later, I managed to find Mr. Jensen through a series of phone calls to gallery owners in the Boston area. A man named Levine told me that Jensen was now retired, but still occasionally dealt in paintings. "His house is a treasure trove," he said.

When I got Jensen on the phone, I said, "Let me tell you a crazy story," and I proceeded to tell him about Léger's toothache and the history of the painting.

"I remember it very well," he said when I'd finished. "Personally, I didn't like it. But I knew Ricci, and I knew I could sell it."

"Do you remember who offered it to you?"

"I'm afraid not," he replied. "Fifteen years is a long time. But I still have my files. If you'll hold on..." I waited twenty minutes on the line. Twice he came back to tell me, "Don't hang up, I'm coming closer," then, the third time, he said, "Got it... Mark Kumin and Sarah Halper."

"Both? You're sure?"

"It's right here — they both signed the forms."

"And no one else?" I was thinking of my youngest sister Florence.

"No one."

"Do you have the date of their contract with you?"

"June 17, 1987."

So they'd hidden away the painting for three years before putting it on the market.

"Do you mind telling me the price?" I asked.

"Oh, it was a bargain. Two hundred and seventy-five thousand. Minus my commission, of course."

After I hung up, I sat for a long time with my head buzzing. For maybe a hundred thousand dollars each, Mark and Sarah had stolen our father's painting; been willing to let lies about me go unchallenged; and never spoken with me again. It didn't make much sense. And Florence? Had she been involved behind the scenes? I suspected so. She was clever enough to have developed the plan and found a way around actually signing anything.

I couldn't sleep that night. The sheets were icy, the bed too small. I watched TV and thought about the past as if I were searching for clues to a murder. At nine the next morning, I called Mr. Ricci back and asked if I could see the painting. He explained that he was an old man, seventy-seven, and was no longer in the habit of receiving guests.

"I'll come whenever you want and I'll only stay a

moment," I said. He simply sighed, so I added, "I'll pay you five hundred dollars just to stand in front of it for a minute."

"Oh dear, that won't be necessary," he answered in an apologetic tone. "How about tomorrow, say early afternoon?"

His granddaughter got on the phone to give me directions to his house. That night, I fished out my father's old medicines from the bottom of my linen closet and took a Valium in order to sleep. In the morning, I rented a car and drove to Princeton. I'd never been there before. Ricci lived in a wealthy neighbourhood with towering oaks and perfect lawns about a mile west of the University. His house was English Tudor. When I rang the bell, a young woman answered. She introduced herself as the granddaughter I'd spoken to. She was tiny, with short brown hair. She wore jeans and a baggy woolen sweater. When I thanked her for giving me such good directions, she smiled warmly. "My grandfather is waiting for you with the painting," she said.

I'm usually quite observant, but I have no idea even today what the foyer looked like or how exactly we got to the living room. I suddenly couldn't seem to get my breath, and I was worried that I was going to faint. All I remember is my feet pounding on a wooden floor for the longest time. Then, I saw Ricci seated in a wheelchair at the centre of a large, brightly lit room, with all the walls painted white. He was bald and shrunken. A blue blanket was draped over his shoulders. He was holding my father's Léger in his skeletal hands. He smiled, and I remember his teeth were too large.

"Is this the painting, Professor Kumin?" he asked.

I nodded.

Objects must soak up memory and become aligned to certain events; looking at the Léger, I was overwhelmed with the feeling of being with my mother. It was as if we were about to play a game of gin rummy on her bed.

It was then that I understood why the painting meant so very much to my father, and why I'd discovered him once sleeping with it on his lap.

"Professor Kumin, would you like to take a closer look?" Ricci asked.

When he held it out to me, a hollow ache opened in my gut. I wanted to run my finger over her hair, but I was sure I'd burst into tears if I did.

"No, thank you," I whispered. "I think I should get going."

I turned and rushed past Ricci's granddaughter out of the living room. While running to my car, she called my name once, but I didn't turn around. I cursed myself for having visited.

At home I went through old photographs of my parents. I kept looking at my mother as if there were a mark I needed to find — later, I figured I was looking for the first sign of her cancer. Then I had this overwhelming urge to see her grave. I felt like a character in some feverish detective novel. So I drove out to Roslyn and found the Mt. Sinai cemetery. It was past closing time. The sun was setting, and the gates were locked. But the brick wall around the cemetery was only four feet high. On hoisting myself over, I found scruffy lawns, pink azalea bushes, and neat rows of white marble headstones. I rushed around like a trespasser till I found my parents' graves. It took less time than I thought, maybe a half hour. By then, dusk had veiled everything a solemn grey.

Isadore Kumin
January 12, 1903–June 18, 1984

Gnendl Rosencrantz Kumin,
December 4, 1906–June 6, 1954.

I gathered pebbles and put them on their headstones and kept putting them there till there was no space left for anything. Then I put some more stones in my coat pockets till they felt heavy enough for me to leave.

When I got home, I typed one-line notes to each of my three siblings: "I know now for sure that you stole Dad's painting."

It seemed important to let them know that I had found out about their treachery, but not to say anything more.

Florence was the only one to write me back. She sent a typed, single-spaced, seventeen page letter. She wrote about all the bad things my father and I had ever done to her. Eleven times she told me that I was a "queer without balls" and that if I'd had any courage I would have admitted years ago that I'd done everything I could to ruin her life. I had the feeling that she typed the letter with a hammer in each hand. A lot of incidents she referred to were totally invented: *Don't you remember how you and Dad abandoned me after Mom's death. And then when you made fun of me for having an abortion when you knew I had no way of raising a baby... It was too much to ever forgive.*

The madness shrieking from her pages frightened me, but I couldn't stop reading. On page twelve, I learned more about why she, Mark and Sarah had stolen the Léger. She said that when she was in high school, they'd pleaded with our mother to leave our father and divorce him: *Mom was so good and kind, but you weren't old enough to know. And Dad was evil, a secret man of silent plans whose very presence was toxic....*

When their effort failed, and when our mother died, Florence realised that she couldn't bear to see our father keep "The Woman with Stone Hair": *We had to get the portrait of Mom away from him. He had her in life, but would never keep her in death. I had to make sure of that. And we knew you wouldn't agree, so we never told you.*

***

When I was growing up, I always thought that as an adult I'd be friends with my siblings, particularly Florence. I also thought that as we age we must each inevitably grow more accepting of our parents and their failings.

Over the last three nights, I've gotten calls at two in the morning, but when I answer, no one is there. The last time it happened, I had enough of my wits to say, "Florence, if this is you, then please don't call again."

Sometimes, in my dreams, I see her trapped in one of Léger's *espaces fermées* — closed spaces. She kicks and screams, but she can't get out. Even so, I'm not taking any chances. I changed my phone number today and workmen are coming over in the morning to install a security system.

True Short Stories

Ali Smith

There were two men in the cafe at the table next to mine. One was younger, one was older. They could have been father and son, but there was none of that practised diffidence, none of the cloudy anger that there almost always is between fathers and sons. Maybe they were the result of a parental divorce, the father keen to be a father now that his son was properly into his adulthood, the son keen to be a man in front of his father now that his father was opposite him for at least the length of time of a cup of coffee. No. More likely the older man was the kind of family friend who provides a fathership on summer weekends for the small boy of a divorce-family; a man who knows his responsibility, and now look, the boy had grown up, the man was an older man, and there was this unsaid understanding between them etc.

I stopped making them up. It felt a bit wrong to. Instead, I listened to what they were saying. They were talking about literature, which happens to be interesting to me, though it wouldn't interest a lot of people. The younger man was talking about the difference between the novel and the short story.

The novel, he was saying, was a flabby old whore.

"A flabby old whore!" the older man said looking delighted.

"She was serviceable, roomy, warm and familiar," the younger was saying, "but really a bit used up, really a bit too slack and loose."

"Slack and loose!" the older said laughing.

Whereas the short story, by comparison, was a nimble goddess, a slim nymph. Because so few people had mastered the short story she was still in very good shape.

Very good shape! The older man was smiling from ear to ear at this. He was presumably old enough to remember years in his life, and not so long ago, when it would have been at least a bit dodgy to talk like this. I idly wondered how many of the books in my house were fuckable and how good they'd be in bed. Then I sighed, and got my mobile out and phoned my friend, with whom I usually go to this cafe on Friday mornings.

She knows quite a lot about the short story. She's spent a lot of her life reading them, writing about them, teaching them, even on occasion writing them. She's read more short stories than most people know (or care) exist. I suppose you could call it a lifelong act of love, though she's not very old, she's in her late thirties. A life-so-far act of love. But already she knows more about the short story, and about the people all over the world who write and have written short stories, than anyone I've ever met.

She was in hospital on this particular Friday because a course of chemotherapy had destroyed every single one of her tiny white blood cells and after it had she'd picked up an infection in a wisdom tooth.

I waited for the automaton voice of the hospital phone system to tell me all about itself, then to recite robotically back to me the number I'd just called, then to mispronounce robotically my friend's name, which is Kasia, then to tell me exactly how much it was charging me to listen to it tell me

71

all this, and then to tell me how much it would cost to speak to my friend per minute. Then it connected me.

"Hi," I said. "It's me."

"Are you on your mobile?" she said. "Don't, Ali, it's expensive on this system. I'll call you back."

"No worries," I said. "It's just a quickie. Listen. Is the short story a goddess and a nymph and is the novel an old whore?"

"Is what what?" she said.

"An old whore, kind of Dickensian one, maybe, I said. Like that prostitute who first teaches David Niven how to have sex in that book."

"David Niven?" she said.

"You know," I said. "The prostitute he goes to in *The Moon's a Balloon* when he's about fourteen, and she's really sweet and she initiates him and he loses his virginity, and he's still wearing his socks, or maybe that's the prostitute who's still wearing the socks, I can't remember, anyway, she's really sweet to him and then he goes back to see her in later life when she's an old whore and he's an internationally famous movie star, and he brings her lots of presents because he's such a nice man and never forgets a kindness. And is the short story more like Princess Diana?"

"The short story like Princess Diana," she said. "Right. Okay."

I sensed the two men, who were getting ready to leave the cafe, looking at me curiously. I held up my phone.

"I'm just asking my friend what she thinks about your nymph thesis," I said.

Both men looked slightly startled. Then both men left the cafe without looking back.

I told her about the conversation I'd just overheard.

"I was thinking of Diana because she was a bit nymphy, I suppose," I said. "I can't think of a goddess who's like a nymph," I said. "All the goddesses that come into my head are, like, Kali, or Sheel-Na-Gig. Or Aphrodite, she was pretty tough. All that deer-slaying. Didn't she slay deer?"

"Why is the short story like a nymph?" Kasia said. "Sounds like a dirty joke. Ha."

"Okay," I said. "Come on then. Why is the short story like a nymph?"

"I'll think about it," she said. "It'll give me something to do in here."

Kasia and I have been friends now for nearly twenty years, which doesn't feel at all long, though it sounds quite long. 'Long' and 'short' are relative. What was long was every single day she was spending in hospital; today was her tenth long day in one of the cancer wards, being injected with a cocktail of antibiotics and waiting for her temperature to come down and her white cell count to go up. When those two tiny personal adjustments happened in the world, then she'd be allowed to go home. Also, there was a lot of sadness round her in the ward. After ten long days the heaviness of that sadness, which might sound bearably small if you're not a person who has to think about it or is being forced by circumstance to address it, but is close to epic if you are, was considerable.

She phoned me back later that afternoon and left a message on the answerphone. I could hear the clanking hospital and the voices of other people in the background in the ward in the recorded air around her voice.

Okay. Listen to this. It depends what you mean by 'nymph'. So, depending. A short story is like a nymph because satyrs want to sleep with it all the time. A short story is like a nymph because both like to live on mountains and in groves and by springs and rivers and in valleys and cool grottoes. A short story is like a nymph because it likes to accompany

Artemis on her travels. Not very funny yet, I know, but I'm
working on it, I'll get it.

I heard the phone being hung up. Message received at four forty three, my answerphone's robot voice said. I called her back and went through the exact echo of the morning's call to the system. She answered and before I could even say hello she said:

"Listen! Listen! A short story is like a nymphomaniac because both like to sleep around — or get into lots of anthologies — but neither accepts money for the pleasure."

I laughed out loud.

"Unlike the bawdy old whore, the novel, ha ha," she said. "And when I was speaking to my father at lunchtime he told me you can fish for trout with a nymph. They're a kind of fishing fly. He says there are people who carry magnifying glasses around with them all the time in case they get the chance to look at real nymphs, so as to be able to echo them even better in the fishing flies they make."

"I tell you," I said. "The world is full of astounding things."

"I know," she said. "What d'you reckon to the anthology joke?"

"Six out of ten," I said.

"Rubbish then," she said. "Okay. I'll try and think of something better."

"Maybe there's mileage in the nymphs-at-your-flies thing," I said.

"Ha ha," she said. "But I'll have to leave the nymph thing this afternoon and get back on the herceptin trail."

"God," I said.

"I'm exhausted," she said. "We're drafting letters."

"When is an anti-cancer drug not an anti-cancer drug?" I said.

"When people can't afford it," she said. "Ha ha."

"Lots of love," I said.

"You too," she said. "Cup of tea?"

"I'll make us one," I said. "Speak soon."

I heard the phone go dead. I put my end of it down and went through and put the kettle on. I watched it reach the boil and the steam come out of the spout. I filled two cups with boiling water and dropped the teabags in. I drank my tea watching the steam rise off the other cup.

This is what Kasia meant by 'herceptin trail'.

Herceptin is a drug that's been being used in cancer treatment for a while now. Doctors have very recently discovered that it really helps some women who have one particular type of cancer, her, when this type is found in early diagnosis. When given to a receptive case it can cut the risk of the recurrence of cancer by fifty per cent. Doctors all over the world are excited about it. It amounts to a paradigm shift in cancer treatment.

I had never heard of any of this till Kasia told me, and she had never heard of any of it until a small truth, less than two centimetres in size, which a doctor found in April in one of her breasts, had meant a paradigm shift in everyday life. It was now August. In May her doctor had told her about how good herceptin is and how she'd definitely be able to have it at the end of her chemotherapy on the NHS. Then at the end of July her doctor was visited by a member of the PCT, which stands for the words Primary Care and Trust, and is concerned with NHS funding. The PCT member instructed my friend's doctor not to tell any more of the women affected in the hospital's cachement area about the availability of herceptin on the NHS, because the PCT had decided that although herceptin was available all over the world it simply wouldn't be standardly available here till a group called NICE approved its use (which is just another way of saying they were putting it off because of lack of responsibility over who would fund it). Though if anyone wanted to buy it on BUPA, for roughly twenty seven thousand pounds, they could, right now.

'Primary'. 'Care'. 'Trust'. 'Nice'.

Here's a short story that most people already think they know about a nymph. (It also happens to be one of the earliest manifestations in literature of what we now call anorexia.)

Echo was an Oread, which is a kind of mountain nymph. She was well known among the nymphs and shepherds not just for her glorious garrulousness but for her ability to save her nymph friends from the wrath of the goddess Juno. For instance, her friends would be lying about on the hillside in the sun and Juno would come round the corner, about to catch them slacking, and Echo, who had a talent for knowing when Juno was about to turn up, would leap to her feet and head the goddess off by running up to her and distracting her with stories and talk, talk and stories, until all the slacker nymphs were up and working like they'd never been slacking at all.

When Juno worked out what Echo was doing she was a bit annoyed. She pointed at her with her curse-finger and threw off the first suitable curse that came into her head.

"From now on," she said, "you will be able only to repeat out loud the words you've heard others say only a moment before. Won't you?"

"Won't you," Echo said.

Her eyes grew large. Her mouth fell open.

"That's you sorted," Juno said.

"You sordid," Echo said.

"Right. I'm off back to the hunt," Juno said.

"The c★★★," Echo said.

Actually I'm making up that small rebellion. There is actually no rebelliousness for Echo, in Ovid's original version of her story. It seems that after she's robbed of being able to talk on her own terms, and of being able to watch her friends' backs for them, there's nothing left for her — in terms of story — but to fall in love with a boy so in love with himself that he spends all his days bent over a pool of his own desire and eventually pines to near-death (then transforms, instead of dying, from a boy into a little white flower).

Echo pined too. Her weight dropped off her. She became fashionably skinny, then she became nothing but bones, then all that was left of her was a whiny, piny voice which floated bodilessly about saying over and over exactly the same things that everybody else was saying.

Here, by contrast, is the story of the moment I met my friend Kasia, nearly twenty years ago.

I was a postgraduate student at Cambridge and I had lost my voice. I don't mean I'd lost it because I had a cold or a thoat infection, I mean that two years of a system of hierarchies so entrenched that girls and women were still a bit of a novelty to it had somehow knocked what voice I had out of me.

So I was sitting at the back of a room not even really listening properly anymore, and I heard a voice. It was from somewhere up ahead of me. It was a girl's voice and it was directly asking the person giving the seminar and the chair of the seminar a question about the American writer Carson McCullers.

Because it seems to me that McCullers is obviously very relevant at all levels in this discussion, the voice said.

The person and the chair of the meeting both looked a bit shocked that anyone had said anything out loud. The chair cleared his throat.

I found myself leaning forward. I hadn't heard anybody speak like this, with such an open and carefree display of knowledge and forthrightness, for a couple of years. More: earlier that day I had been talking with an undergraduate student who had been unable to find anyone in the whole of Cambridge University English Department to supervise her dissertation on McCullers. It seemed nobody eligible to teach had read her.

Anyway I venture to say you'll find McCullers not at all of the same stature, the person giving the paper on Literature After Henry James said.

"Well, the thing is, I disagree," the voice said.

I laughed out loud. It was a noise never heard in such a room; heads turned to see who was making such an unlikely noise. The new girl carried on politely asking questions which no one answered. She mentioned, I remember, how McCullers had been fond of a maxim: nothing human is alien to me.

At the end of the seminar I ran after that girl. I stopped her in the street. It was winter. She was wearing a red coat.

She told me her name. I heard myself tell her mine.

Franz Kafka says that a short story is a cage in search of a bird. (Kafka's been dead for 81 years, but I can still say Kafka says. That's just one of the ways art deals with our mortality.)

Tzvetan Todorov says that the thing about a short story is that it's so short it doesn't allow us the time to forget that it's only literature and not actually life.

Nadine Gordimer says short stories are absolutely about the present moment, like the brief flash of a number of fireflies here and there in the dark.

Elizabeth Bowen says the short story has the advantage over the novel of a special kind of concentration, and that it creates narrative every time absolutely on its own terms.

Eudora Welty says that short stories often problematise their own best interests and that this is what makes them interesting.

Henry James says that the short story, being so condensed, can give a particularised perspective on both complexity and continuity.

Jorge Luis Borges says that short stories can be the perfect form for novelists too lazy to write anything longer than fifteen pages.

Ernest Hemingway says that short stories are made by their own change and movement, and that even when a story seems static and you can't make out any movement in it at all it is probably changing and moving regardless, just unseen by you.

William Carlos Williams says that the short story, which acts like the flare of a match struck in the dark, is the only real form for describing the briefness, the brokenness and the simultaneous wholeness of people's lives.

Walter Benjamin says that short stories are stronger than the real, lived moment, because they can go on releasing the real, lived moment long after the real, lived moment is dead.

Cynthia Ozick says that the difference between a short story and a novel is that the novel is a book whose journey, if it's a good working novel, actually alters a reader, whereas a short story is more like the talismanic gift given to the protagonist of a fairy tale — something complete, powerful, whose power may yet not be understood, which can be held in the hands or tucked into the pocket and taken through the forest on the dark journey.

Grace Paley says that she has written only short stories in her life because art is too long and life is too short, and that short stories are, by nature, about life, and that life is itself always found in dialogue and argument.

Alice Munro says that every short story is at least two short stories.

There were two men in the cafe at the table next to mine. One was younger, one was older. We sat in the same cafe for only a brief amount of time but we disagreed for long enough for me to know there was a story in it.

This story has been written in discussion with my friend Kasia Boddy (39), writer, lecturer and critic, who happens at this live moment to be one of the 2,000 women in the UK who will have to pay for a drug they should all simply be eligible for — no argument — right now.

So when is the short story like a nymph?

When the echo of it answers back.

Not The End of All

Nicole Krauss

The other day I met my friend at the Bombay Club, across from the White House. I was the first to arrive. I was carrying Max Brod's biography of Kafka in my bag, and while I waited among the palms fronds, shutters, and brass ceiling fans, I pretended to read. When my friend arrived he was wearing a coat, a wide-brimmed olive felt hat, and large aviator sunglasses. The only parts of him that protruded from this disguise were his nose and the ends of his thick white hair. We embraced the way people do when they haven't seen each other for years, but in the meantime have written many letters.

In fact, I'd only met him in person once before — I live in New York, and only rarely go to D.C. — and it seemed to me now, looking at him across the table, that he'd aged since then. His son, who then had been only a few months old, was now three and a half. Before we'd even ordered — or before my friend ordered for us, because he took the initiative, suggesting I get a special shrimp curry dish eaten by the Zoroastrians for the New Year — my friend told me about his immense love for his son, and how he didn't think of him as his offspring, but rather someone entirely other, a separate being utterly surprising and delightful in every way. "The things that come out of his mouth," my friend said. I asked him to give me an example. "The other day it snowed. When we woke up the ground was covered. I was putting my son's jacket on before school, and he stopped and smiled, and quoted to me a line from a book I sometimes read to him before bed. He didn't refer to the story; he simply quoted the line without context, which anyway is unnecessary between us. 'Daddy,' he said to me. 'Something is wrong with the world.' That was the line. And I said, 'My son, you have no idea.'"

Two plates of appetisers arrived. I helped myself from one, and only as the fish landed on my plate did it occur to me that it would have been kind to serve my friend first. Quickly I felt even worse, because he proceeded to serve me from the other appetiser before helping himself, and the gesture seemed so full of generosity that I wanted to bite my shirt, and only further, more eradicable embarrassment kept me from doing so. A few moments into our meal, the maitre d' came over to say hello to my friend, who dines often at the Bombay Club, and as he approached our table my friend happened to be in the middle of telling me, very candidly, about how he'd given up his habit of bullshitting — something I'd heard of, but never seen any evidence of myself, since he'd given up this particular self-described habit long before I met him, and because, despite an almost divine verbal facility, his presence holds the tenderness and weight of someone who has been engaged in a lifelong struggle. When I asked him why he'd finally changed, whether it was because he'd reached a certain age, my friend said, "No — the death of my father, the birth of my son, fifty years since Auschwitz — no, none of that is why I gave it up, I simply became — " but he didn't finish his sentence because just then the maitre d' arrived to inform my friend, with a small, effacing bow, that the special shrimp dish was back on the menu by popular demand.

As we ate, my friend mentioned a picture of me he had seen somewhere, and told me that he had known the photographer for thirty-five years. I'd known her for only three, but just as with my friend, she and I had struck a deep and immediate chord, and our feeling for each other surpassed the brevity of our friendship. We'd met for the first time a few days after September 11th. Some weeks earlier we'd arranged for her to take my portrait, but now the task seemed small and petty. I called her to discuss cancelling, but in the end we decided that it would be good for us to work. On September 14th I went to her apartment downtown, a large loft on the top floor of a Victorian building that seemed to have remained unchanged for decades, aside from the slow but constant accumulation of things the photographer brought home from the flea market. Edith Piaf was singing on the stereo, and with its peeling paint and enormous mullioned windows looking out on the mansard, the place had the feel of something abandoned by time. As a rule, I don't like having my picture taken, for one thing because I never know what to do with my hands. But on that day, my hands and where to put them, like everything else, seemed unimportant. Eventually we went up onto the roof, and when the wind blew a certain way it brought the stench of burning fuel and flesh, so particular to those days right after the collapse of the Towers. Now, as we ate our Zoroastrian New Year's dish, my friend told me how beautiful the photographer had been as a young woman, and how when they first met, after spending a day in each other's company, she often would send him a little book of photographs of all the things they'd discovered together. Then he told me something that in my many conversations with her she'd never once mentioned. She only had one love in life, my friend said, and one night she went out, and the place they lived together caught fire, and he died.

We spoke, either then or later, about self-loathing, which he warned me was a precious commodity that should be guarded as closely as possible, and soon, though not directly afterwards, he described how years ago he'd been reading George Orwell, and he came to the line *Viewed from the inside, everything is worse.* "And as I read," he said, "it hit me how true it was, and that there was no exception to that rule."

Over the course of our lunch, my friend and I spoke of many things. We sat for so long that the restaurant, which had been full when we arrived, emptied, and the angle of light coming through the shutters shifted. He asked me where my family came from — "Who are you?" he said, half joking, which is the only kind of joking there is — and as I answered I found myself involuntarily quoting almost verbatim from an essay I'd recently written about my grandparents, making me feel uneasy, as if I'd rehearsed the very same conversation already and now were only acting a role.

The week before, I'd taken a trip to Venice. Over the course of our letters I'd asked my friend the meaning of the Latin inscription on the headstone of another mutual friend of ours, who was buried there, on St. Michele. The inscription was short, and my friend had written to me that it was from Book IV, 7 of Propertius' Elegies, the one where he is visited by Cynthia's ghost. Now, as we got up to go, he handed me a manila envelope with a photocopy of the elegy, because that's the sort of person he is. As I put it into my bag he saw the Kafka biography, and the conversation about gravestones moved out of the restaurant and into the chilly February sunlight, where he told me that he had in his possession a rubbing of Kafka's gravestone. As we turned the corner and passed the White House, he described a trip he'd taken to Prague when he was young. One night he'd gotten completely sloshed, and become convinced that he needed to go out and kiss the AlteNeue Shul, directly across the street from where he was staying. The next morning he woke up unharmed, still embracing the *shul*, perhaps watched over by the remains of the golem supposedly buried in the attic. That afternoon he decided to go to the Jewish Straschnitz Cemetery to visit Kafka. "He was buried next to his father, which was more or less the worst insult I could imagine," my friend said. "I decided I was going to say Kaddish for Kafka," he said. "So I did. When I was finished I turned to go, and standing there behind me was the exact same headstone. I stood there, bewildered. A few minutes later some kids sauntered in and explained that they'd just finished a replica of Kafka's headstone for a movie that was being shot, and had left it there while they went to lunch. I'd said Kaddish to the replica. I helped them load it into their truck. The rubbing they'd done of the real stone was sitting there, and I asked them if I could have it."

As my friend spoke we approached the office where he works when he isn't teaching Maimonides on creation, miracles, and natural law, and he invited me up to see the rubbing. Between the restaurant and his office, a vague feeling of sadness had come over me, mixed in and impossible to separate from the pleasure of finally being in my friend's company. Maybe it was from so much talk of death, or how he'd said that not a month went by when he didn't think of, and miss, the company of the poet buried in Venice, who I also missed in my own way, and whose headstone is inscribed with the words, *Letum non omnia finit*.

His office was large and filled, as I'd expected, with books. Propped up against the rows of spines were an assortment of postcards and photographs. Among these was the rubbing of Kafka's grave. It was in Hebrew, and my friend read it aloud and translated it to me. In it, Kafka was called by his Hebrew name, as Jews are always called in birth and death. Kafka's was Anschel, a name I'd never heard before, and when I asked about it my friend explained that in fact it was Yiddish. This led to a discussion of both of our Hebrew names, and to the Hebrew name of his son. He asked me who I was named for, and I told him it was my great aunt Dora, who died in the Warsaw ghetto, and then we discussed how it goes without saying that one's Hebrew name is after someone to whom something sad has happened; sometimes merely death, and sometimes a tragic death. "This is what they don't understand in America," my friend said, who was born in Brooklyn. "When you ask them why they've named their child something, they always answer, 'Because I liked it.' Who names their children something just because they like it?" As he spoke, he inscribed to me a copy of one of his books, in which he'd written that the hardest thing in America is to be what one is softly.

The next day, on the drive back to New York, I found myself unable to escape the feeling that I'd failed to ask him for advice about something important. As I drove, I listened to the radio, first a program about Sarah Vaughan, and then the news, a man wanted for a string of fatal jewelry store robberies, who finally handed himself over to the police after holing up with his girlfriend in a hotel in Atlantic City for three days. I thought about that for awhile, and then for miles of New Jersey I wondered about the photographer: how often she thought of her only love, and the many things she'd never gotten around to asking him.

Once she'd come to my house in Brooklyn and we decided to go up to the roof to see the view of lower Manhattan. She was nervous about climbing the old and rickety ladder, but did it anyway. At the top it was so bright that we had to squint. The seat of her pants got dirty, and she

86

almost lost her glasses. In the photograph she snapped of me that day you can't tell if I'm laughing or crying. Now that I think about it, I've spent more time on roofs with her than with anyone I've ever met.

Jewish Values

Michelene Wandor

My name is Sarah and this is my life story. That was how I
began the diary. My name, of course, isn't Sarah, and I have
never written a diary. Perhaps that was why the idea appealed
to me so much. I never wrote a diary because I thought my
life was pretty boring. If you think your life is really boring,
then inevitably you will imagine that everyone else's life is
much more exciting. Or at least exciting. Or at the very least,
more interesting.

Life as an academic is boring. Don't listen to what anyone
tells you about the long holidays, the delight in long, silent
sessions in the library, poring over books, seeking out dusty
old manuscripts, making new discoveries, giving the world
new knowledges. In the spanking new British Library on the
Euston Road you are only allowed to take pencils into the
Rare Manuscripts room, for fear you might deface one of the
precious items only to be read in that room. It was just such
a pencil, carefully sharpened before I began work one day,
which triggered everything.

I used to love working in the British Library, though I was
always disconcerted when I approached the building. I
thought it looked like a cross between an oriental temple and
a concentration camp building. Once inside, however, my
associations were entirely with the idea of a temple — the

calm, the privacy and excitement of communing with writing on the page, a private light for each reader, power points for laptop computers. The interruptions of bell-like signals, as other members of the congregation turn their machines on and off were like the sounds of random calls to prayer.

And yet the concentration camp connection haunted me. Not, I hasten to add, because of the building per se, though there was (still is) something about the monolithic frontage, the long, solid brick lines at the side of the building. Perhaps a distant memory of my father showing me photographs of the camp buildings. Not because he had lost any of this family this way — he was already third generation born in London. But, as with the rest of us, the horrors experienced by others became his own fears for the worst.

On a good day, with the sun shining brightly on the stone and glimmering from the red-painted parts of the façade, I could equally well imagine that the library was really a 21st century railway station, cheek by jowl with the newly refurbished gothic vampire Frankenstein redbrick, Cadbury's flake chocolate of St Pancras, and its neighbour monster expansion of Kings Cross. Here Eurostar was being welcomed, after nosing its way under the Channel and up to northern London.

These flights of fancy are something of a compensation at the edges of the life of an academic. In between these speculations, in between reading books and marking student essays, coping with classes which were too large and students who were too lazy (with the occasional exception), the life of an academic really is parasitic, secondary. I worried over books which other people had worried over for centuries. I wrote more articles and more books, hoping, determined, to say something different, something undiscovered, something exegetical, to add to bodies of knowledge and further my own career. And I was very successful in the latter. I was made a Professor before I reached the age of thirty — a rare event in a profession with a carefully demarcated ladder of career progression.

My father was delighted. At my degree ceremony, he kissed me on both cheeks and whispered his congratulations. You beat them at their own game, he said. I didn't fully understand this until later, at a family party, when he insisted that I should wear my mortar board for the photographs in the garden. He repeated the phrase. You beat them at their own game. Them? I asked — who is them. Them, he said, them, them, them. You beat them at their own game. I don't think of it that way, I said. Ah, he said. You'll understand one day. Jewish values. Beat the *goyim* at their own game. Show them that you are as clever as them, and if at all possible, cleverer than them.

For a moment I thought this might finally help him to understand why I no longer had any interest in the Jewish religion. But no. He continued: that's why we must keep ourselves apart. One day they may turn on you for being cleverer than they are. I had drunk quite a lot of champagne by then, and didn't feel my younger need to argue with him. Besides, my family really were pleased and I didn't want to spoil the show.

I never could admit to my parents that I found the academic life so tedious. They would not have understood why I did not simply bask in my success and achievement. They did. They displayed my books on their shelves; they didn't need to read them.

And so, in a way, this takes me back to where I started. My name is Sarah and this is my life story. Thus began the manuscript, newly discovered in a private library in Venice. The loosely bound pages were in spidery handwriting, in an archaic Hebrew hand, fluent and surprisingly modern. The diary entries were interspersed with short poems. My own

Hebrew, never officially used in my work as an English Literature academic, had been acquired and honed in a progressive *cheder*, which took in girls as well as boys. This was all before the progressivising of Judaism took England by ministorm. No bat-mitzvahs, or if there were (as there was for me) undertaken almost in private, with little public display, and only a *minyan* of close friends and relatives to sanction the ceremony (yes, the *minyan* was still all male).

The bat-mitzvah was a signal to me, a watershed, a clarion call, to use clichés I would veto from any student essay. After the service, I stopped going anywhere near anything Jewish. Fierce arguments with my father when I refused to go to *shul*, threats to throw me out of the house when I yelled that I would never marry a Jewish man (and I didn't), and bewildered distress from both parents when I told them as gently as I could that my son would not be circumcised. The word "assimilated" was never uttered, but it hovered behind all my visits home for some years. A silent accusation that I had abandoned the fold, the tribe, and gone to live with the aliens, adopting their culture, their beliefs, their values. Not Jewish values.

Until, that is, my son charmed them so much with his fascination for things Jewish, that my sin was swept under the carpet (to use another cliché which, etc, etc). He did tell them that his interest was cultural, rather than religious, but they never really understood the distinction. It didn't matter to them, anyway. He wanted to know about Judaism, and they jumped at the chance to tell him.

So it was ironic when the prime mover behind my extraordinary career appointment was Jewish, and reconciled my father to me. Sarah Costa was a Venetian poet, who lived during the first part of the 17th century. It was claimed that she held a regular cultural salon, where writers, painters, musicians and any old intellectual would gather.

I had finished my PhD efficiently, in the required three years, outstripping my colleagues who all laboured on for years more. I published my first monograph, on Henry James, at twenty-seven. I had discovered an unpublished short story of his, which surprised and outraged James scholars, who thought they knew it all. I didn't see myself as a James scholar — I had chosen him for my PhD as a judicious, respectable scholarly choice, and secured me one of the foremost Jamesian scholars as my Cambridge supervisor. My book contained versions of all six drafts of the story, commenting on the editing and rewriting choices, producing a learned, variorum edition.

The book was reviewed by all the respectable literary and scholarly publications in the country, and in America. None of this made any difference to my parents, of course. What did they know, or want to know, from Henry James? Henry? What kind of a man, joked my mother once, is so indecisive about his name that he has to choose two first names? She carefully avoided saying "Christian".

On the strength of the book, I was offered an academic job in one of the more prestigious new universities of the 1960s. I was delighted. My parents were delighted. I had a good salary. My parents were overjoyed. I found a one-bedroom flat in a suburb. My father helped me with the down-payment. The only thing which would have pleased them even more would have been if I had also found myself a nice Jewish husband, who could provide for me. Then I would not have needed the job, the salary, or the flat. But worldly success was important. As long as we kept our Jewish values, etc, etc.

Then I fell in love, to my great surprise. Up till then, the fact that I had no love life (curious euphemism for sex, I've always thought) really hadn't worried me. It still didn't, but falling in love really did surprise me. Particularly because the man was Jewish. Looking back, it probably wasn't so suprising. Although my intellectual and academic work was up there with the best of them, I was what people call "shy". I'm not shy at all really, but I didn't know the lingo. I had not been to public school, and I simply felt uncomfortable in the presence of all these highly cultured and well spoken people.

I have since met many Jewish intellectuals, men and women, who look and talk as if they too have come through the public school system, who are indistinguishable from the cultured English. They "pass" without even trying. They don't have to pass — they are, they think, accepted. What they don't know is that very occasionally someone, behind their back, will refer to them as "that little Jew", that "beautiful Jewess", that "clever little Jew". Because I am shy and relatively unobtrusive, and because the English can be incredibly rude in ignoring people they don't think are worth talking to, I would sometimes be privy to such remarks, made supposedly, quietly. This was at odds with my public, professional, persona; sure, confident in lectures, gracious and articulate on official occasions, enthusiastic and inspirational with my students.

Anyway, there he was: this Jewish man from Australia. The relationship didn't last long, but long enough for me to become pregnant. By the time my son was born (prematurely, for the family record), I was married to a nice, non-Jewish academic (public school, etc), who privately thought he had rescued me from the horrors of illegitimate motherhood. My parents were so relieved that the marriage made me respectable, that they said hardly anything about the sparse, registry-office ceremony, and, to my amazement, nothing about his non-Jewishness. Perhaps my father still thought I was beating them at their own game: marrying in, rather than marrying out; being an intellectual Trojan horse, rather than assimilating.

From that moment, however, I found the job boring. I had an office of my own. A department to run. A son to bring up, especially when my husband left me for a younger, student model, before I had even stopped breast feeding. I had never made my office into a home away from home, as many academics do. The office was never my sanctuary. Just somewhere to centre my presence, and to receive students. I never lost the enthusiasm for my subject which gave me a hotline to enthusing my students. I knew that applications to study with me, to be supervised by me, outstripped those of other literature staff. It was a pleasure to me to give my knowledge and critical perceptions and reading to my students, and observe their development. This has never left me.

But the rest began to haunt me. After Professor, then what? I was Henry Jamesed out. I published an occasional book, on some minor nineteenth-century novelists, but my heart wasn't in it. Five years into my Professorship, I reread a Henry James novel, and could not understand what had led my enthusiasm for this dry as dust writing. More recently, I have re-reversed my opinion again, but the point is that at the time, it took me into a new direction.

I left my literary research, and learned Italian. At first for my own pleasure. It was private and no-one knew. Then time moved on, and suddenly (or so it seemed) I hadn't published anything new for ten years. Universities had become harsher, run like businesses.

I was summoned by the Dean. A gentle, but firm warning. They might have to "lose" me, if my publication record did not step up. Did I have some work nearing fruition and publication. In the shock of the moment, I blurted out the first thing that came into my head. I have been researching 17th century poetry in Venice, I said, and I have made an extraordinary discovery. The Dean was relieved and busy, and happy to wave me away, to get on with my new research.

There wasn't any, of course. So I forged the first page of a diary and a poem. On the strength of it, I made an extraordinary discovery. Sarah Costa had had affairs with the Doge of Venice, and one of the city's foremost rabbis, Leone da Modena. She had two children, and did not know who the father was of either. This, I argued, came out as evidence from the poem, which was undoubtedly autobiographical. Not that I believe that any poem is really autobiographical, but I wanted my discovery to seep beyond the academic esoteric world, and into the social and vexed worlds of religion and history. It suited me to revert to an old-fashioned, reassuring line of literary criticism. Here was a Jewish woman, a poet, a hostess for intellectual gatherings, to which all came, of whatever religion, Catholic or Jew, and who had even had very close relationships with some of them.

She was a bridge, I claimed, between the Jewish and the Catholic worlds and cultures. Her children were its legacies, and this poem its proof. She reconciled religious differences and different cultural values. She showed what was possible from a distance of several hundred years.

On the strength of this, I was made a Reader, and that is where I remained until my retirement last year. Now. Certain questions will, of course, occur to you. Did anyone examine my documents? Test the paper for authenticity? The ink? The handwriting? The Italian? Unfortunately, there was little evidence to test. Just some fragments of paper, a little like the Dead Sea Scrolls. There had been an unfortunate fire. The villa in which I had "found" this manuscript had a serious fire in its upper rooms. I had visited the villa, and taken a photograph of a couple of pages, intending to return the following week, to borrow the complete manuscript for my research. The fire rendered that impossible. All I had to show for my labours was a photograph of two pages, taken in less than perfect light.

And that is more or less the end of the story. My photograph was framed and is in the university rare manuscripts department. My confession will harm no-one. My scholarly achievements may be discredited, but, as I have already said, I am retired, and it makes no difference. My parents will not be embarrassed or disappointed, for they are both dead. I could, perhaps, even have had a joke with my father. I beat them at their own game, Dad, I'd have said. I forged a document and conned them all, on their own terms. Jewish values. But you lied about this Jewish girl, my father would have said. She had — excuse me — sexual — intimate relations with a Catholic and a rabbi? Why not, I would have answered? Why not? Why not? What do you mean, why not, would have remonstrated my father. Is this kind of behaviour what you call Jewish values?

It's not a question I would ever have wanted to answer.

Boiling
Tania Hershman

They sat with the red light hanging from the tree and the sound of falling mangoes. Skinny cats from the *moshav* slunk around chair legs and water fell in a steady stream from a hose strung among the pomellos. Tomorrow the others would arrive and the little house would be overrun; tonight was theirs alone. Traffic rushed faintly in the distance towards Tiberius, blurred by the thick heat of the night.

Brad took another drag on his roll-up and blew smoke towards his bare feet, up on the corner of the table. Melissa stared up at the full moon. Conrad picked at the skin around his thumbnail.

"Did I ever tell you I met an angel in Cornwall," said Brad, taking another drag. The sound of his voice made Melissa jump. She stared at him, her wide eyes even wider in the darkness.

"When were you in Cornwall," she said, and her own voice sounded deep and unfamiliar. *Cornwall*, she whispered to herself. *Corn. Wall.*

"I was walking along the coast, last year, you remember. I went to get away from it all, stayed in a strange bed and breakfast run by that creepy couple."

"The doughnut-makers," said Conrad, and Brad and Melissa turned towards him. They sometimes forgot Conrad was with them, he said so little, one of those strange quiet Americans who had been in Israel for ten years but hadn't really absorbed anything of the local exuberance. You never quite knew what Conrad was thinking and he often startled you when he spoke, but Melissa liked him anyway. She looked at Brad, trying to share the joke, but the blackness cut her off from him. A cat meowed desperately underneath the table. Melissa meowed back and it shot off into the undergrowth.

"Oh god, yes, I forgot about that." Brad's laugh echoed into the trees. "Freaks," he said. "Anyway, I went strolling, and was sitting on a bench by some little Cornish port, stroking a huge ginger cat…"

"Sounds beautiful," said Melissa.

"And this guy just stopped and started talking to me. He's an artist. Somewhere local. But he started talking to me about love."

"Love?" said Melissa. "What did he say?" She sat forward and started playing with wax that had dripped onto the table earlier, when they had eaten dinner by candlelight. She picked it off with her thumbnail and started massaging it into a ball. Conrad watched the shadows of her fingers moving.

"I can't really remember it in detail. All I remember thinking was that he was talking about me, about exactly what I had just been through with Eleanor, and I couldn't understand how he knew all that."

"Lucky guess," said Conrad.

"No," said Brad. "No, it was more than that, more, I don't know, specific. About two people loving each other but not being able to be together, something always coming between them, and knowing when to give up, even though it hurts."

"God," said Melissa. "That's deep."

"Yes, it really was. And it made me feel better. Afterwards, I decided he was an angel, sent to me to tell me everything would be alright, that I would meet someone, some day." Brad dragged deeply on the tiny remains of his roll-up and exhaled with a sigh. Melissa stopped playing with the wax and moved her chair closer to him. She put a hand on his feet, feeling their warmth. She hoped he wasn't thinking about Eleanor.

A mango fell with a thud and Conrad giggled. Melissa suddenly felt cold. She got up and went into the house, turning on the outside light. The men blinked at the world emerging from the blackness.

"Drink?" said Conrad, leaning towards the whisky. Brad pushed his glass over, and they sat in silence, sipping.

Melissa switched on the kettle. The others teased her for drinking tea in this heat, but tea had always been Melissa's comfort: hot, sweet, strong English tea, brought over every time she went back to London to visit or, if no visit was planned, she cajoled a friend to send it by post. Brad had laughed at her when they arrived for making tea even before she unpacked. She told him Americans could never understand, and inside she pretended he wasn't laughing at her so much as enjoying her quirkiness. The kettle boiled and Melissa poured, thinking about Eleanor. About Eleanor and her: her eyes, Eleanor's eyes; her legs, Eleanor's legs; her breasts, one always bigger than the other, and Eleanor's breasts, perfect and identical. When they first met, at Melissa's own birthday party two years ago, she felt sick. She had invited Brad, a new friend, Conrad's friend, and invited him on his own. How dare he bring someone? How dare he bring her, this Amazonian, exploding with health and white teeth, as tanned as Melissa was pale, as strong as Melissa felt pathetic.

Eleanor was lovely, of course, but Melissa dismissed her. When they split up, Melissa rejoiced inside.

Conrad sat and felt the whisky rasp down his throat. Another mango fell with a thud and he suppressed the urge to laugh. He stared at Brad, who was resting his head on the back of his chair and looking up at the stars, smoking. Conrad watched the red of the cigarette move between Brad's mouth and out again into the dark. He imagined the fine blond hairs on the back of Brad's neck which Conrad had gazed at from the back seat of the car as they drove up from Jerusalem through the Bikaa Valley. He had to stop himself from reaching out to stroke them.

They had stopped off at Belvoir Castle.

"It's on our way," Conrad said when they had been in the car for half an hour and were driving through the hills outside Jerusalem. "It's a Crusader ruin. The best preserved Crusader fort. It was captured by Saladin in the 12th century."

"We'll go, sounds great," said Brad. "We Americans never get to see any real ruins, except, you know, when people bomb us, right Con?" Conrad nodded, smiling slightly. Melissa wasn't sure if she wanted to go and walk around a ruin in the heat of the afternoon, but it seemed that they had made the decision for her.

The fort was in its own national park. They paid the old man 18 shekels each at the gate and drove into the parking lot. They got out of the car and the heat hit them like a wave, a humid shimmering heat which blurred all edges.

"Wow," said Melissa. "I'm sweating already." Conrad sniggered. They walked over the reconstructed bridge over the moat.

"'The moat was the first obstacle with which an attacking army would be confronted as it charged the gates,'" Brad read from the pamphlet. Melissa looked down.

"Was there water in it?" she said.

"Oh sure," said Brad. Conrad walked on ahead. Melissa watched him disappear through an archway.

"Come on," said Brad. "Let's see where these Crusaders dropped hot oil on everybody."

Conrad stood on the lookout and tried to see an eagle. This was "Eagle Point", but Conrad saw only cactuses growing out from the sides of the valley below, weighed down with sabra fruit. *Three o'clock in the afternoon must be a bad time for seeing eagles,* he thought. *They're probably having a siesta.* Conrad wondered if the place they were going had firm beds. He would be happy with a mattress on the floor, as long as it was hard. Melissa's sister had been coming to this house by the Kinneret for years with her kids. Melissa said it was a "great space, but don't expect luxury". Conrad hadn't known what to make of that but he didn't really care. He liked being with Melissa, she reminded him of his sister. When she had invited him he didn't ask who else was going, but he had hoped it was Brad.

"This is where they poured the oil," said Brad, standing under an arch and looking up. "There are two arches, and a gap between them. The enemy came up here and then, Wham bam, all fried."

Melissa laughed.

"Just liked chips."

"French fries, you mean," said Brad in his terrible English accent.

"Dick Van Dyke," said Melissa. "You're all hopeless at it, stick to your own tongue."

"My tongue,"said Brad. "It's a nice one."

Melissa went red and turned away to look out over the valley.

"That's Jordan," she said. "It's right there."

Brad's cell phone beeped. He took it out of his pocket.

"I've got a message in Hebrew," he said, and laughed. "God, it says that I'm using a Jordanian cellphone network and I should know that it's more expensive than the Israeli one!"

"Wow, we really are close," said Melissa, staring at the tiny Jordanian villages in the distance at the foot of the mountains. "Maybe you'll get your phone bill in dinars."

She turned round and Brad flashed her a big grin.

"Where's Connie? Come on." He wandered over to the little doorway into the inner fortress rooms and held out his hand to help her climb the ruined steps. She stood and looked at him for a minute, then came towards him and took his hand.

The park closes at four, the old man had told Melissa, who had the best Hebrew. The gate shuts, he said, don't be late. Brad and Melissa were standing on the bridge over the moat when Conrad appeared from around the side of the fortress and wandered over to them. No-one spoke as they walked back to the car. On their way down the hill back to the main road, Brad said,

"Cool fort. Thanks Con."

Conrad nodded.

In the car, Melissa said, "I love old stones. Touching something they touched in the twelfth century. It's amazing."

"At least they haven't turned it into a shopping mall," said Brad, turning sharply out onto the 90 without looking at the oncoming traffic.

Melissa took her tea back outside. She noticed the whisky glasses and wondered if they had been waiting for her to leave before they opened the bottle. She didn't like whisky but it would have been nice to be offered some.

"Good stuff?" She said, gesturing towards the empty glasses.

"Better than drinking boiling water with a couple of dead leaves in it when its two hundred degrees outside," said Brad, and Conrad sniggered.

"Drinking boiling water is better than having it poured on you from the ramparts," said Melissa, blowing on her cup and setting it down on the plastic table.

"Oil," said Conrad.

"Boiling oil, then. Whatever."

Melissa sat down by Brad, who was rolling himself another cigarette. Conrad watched Brad's fingers knead the wisps of tobacco into cigarette shape.

"What shall we do tomorrow?" said Brad, and licked the sticky end of the cigarette paper.

"Depends when they get here. They're all coming in one car," said Melissa. "We could swim."

"Swimming is good," said Conrad.

"Fine," said Melissa.

"Sounds great," said Brad, lighting the cigarette and leaning back again in his chair. "I can't wait 'til the gang get here. Then we'll really party!"

Melissa and Conrad watched him silently. Melissa drank her tea. Conrad refilled his whisky glass.

A cat meowed from beside the barbecue, and somewhere at the back of the garden, a mango fell heavily onto the parched brown grass.

Goals
Jonathan Wilson

The barred owl came flapping out of the trees pursued by a squadron of crows; by day they would not let him alone. The squirrels started to moan with fear and a lone mockingbird sang high in the maple branches. How did I know all this stuff? I mean about the precise species of the owl and the tune of the unfamiliar bird. Because I was standing at the aqueduct with Julian Fazler, my neighbour's fifteen year old son, a boy who was the Stephen Jay Gould of our neighborhood. Neither of us had anything else to do that day. Julian, for reasons associated with his unaffiliated genius, was intermittent at school, while I had recently been relieved of my duties as an advertising executive at Booth&Willis on account of the abject failure (the latest of many) of my "If you can't say it, spray it" campaign for an unpronounceable brand of aerosol paint.

"Look," said Julian, "here he comes again." The owl gave two big wing flaps, as if he was swimming slowly through the air, then he took a glide into the leafy branches of the suburban canopy.

"Time for us to go home," I suggested, "Show's over here."

"Not me," Julian had his binos out, "I'm collecting bark beetles today."

The truth is I was late for my shrink appointment with Dr. Judy Metliss, a meeting that I dreaded because of the stockings issue. Here's what had transpired. In my second week of unemployment I had become emboldened, in the way of those who are euphoric to leave misery and conformity behind them, and decided to tell Dr Metliss about her stockings. We had being going back and forth for a year or so about my resistance to get on the couch (you can hear the Gods of Zoloft and Wellbutrin laughing already). Newly pink-slipped, I hopped on.

"What made you change your mind?" asked the good doctor.

"I can't stand looking at your stockings any longer," I replied.

"Mmm. Hmm."

"Yes. You wear these horrible, unattractive black knee-highs as if you were an Orthodox Jewish wife dragging six kids on each arm, and when the low buttons of your skirt are undone I can see both your fat white knees and the tops of the stockings."

"Why has it taken you so long to tell me this?"

"Because I couldn't tell you to your face."

There was silence in the room until, across the hall where the sane people lived, somebody flushed a toilet.

"OK," I continued, "I've said what I had to say. Now, I'm getting back off this couch."

I had spent the next twenty minutes shivering in the chair, full of shame and remorse.

Had I had to add "fat white?" Wouldn't "knees" have been enough?

Dr Metliss, however, showed remarkable aplomb. After all, as I quickly surmised, she was of the opinion that everything I chucked her way was truly aimed at, guess who? Why, Mommy of course.

"No," I said "this has nothing to do with my mother. It's

about style and fashion. I'm trying to help you."

"And why do you feel so strongly the need to help me?"

It was time to stumble out into the clarifying air. At the corner store on Beacon Street I bought a Diet Coke, five tickets for Mass Millions and a York Peppermint the size of a cartwheel. Nutrasweet and sugar were ancient, well tested and effective tribal cures.

"Winter's here," said my wife Marina as I came in the door. It was September 1. She was scanning the obituaries in the local paper and eating a plum, the juice spread lusciously across her lips. "And there's a phone message for you." When I coded in, the female voice on the other end was upbeat and confident. "Hi JJ, this is Ellen Brody, from FH, you don't know me but Stacey Bortz-Kaplan gave me your number. I have a proposal for you and I hope you'll say yes. Please call either home 617-552-5555 or my cell 617-917-9944 or you can reach me at work..." There were two more numbers.

Bush was on the kitchen counter TV. He had that deer in the headlights look. He was reading three words at a time and trying hard to make it appear that he had thought of them. He was talking about what we owed the dead, and how the only way to pay off the debt was to feed the voracious and insatiable earth more dead.

"Who's Ellen Brody?" I asked.

"How should I know?" my wife replied, "I have no friends."

I dialed one of the work numbers and reached the development office of the Fanny Harper Cancer Institute. The receptionist put me through to Ms B.

"JJ! Here's the dealio. We are a group of soccer moms (*hate* the expression) and we're looking for a coach. I heard that you were the absolute bestest ever with the ten year olds (those twins of yours!) *and* of course everyone knows you have that darling British accent. You *must* know the game. We don't need anything super athletic — more like tips."

"You want me to coach your children?"

"Sweetheart, you sweet thing. We want you to coach *us!*"

After a few moments of conversation I put the phone down and walked back into the kitchen.

"A man died who was 107," Marina said. "He had an operation on his cataracts when he was 100 because he liked to look at the flowers in his window box."

"How did he die?"

"Broken heart syndrome. He couldn't live without his wife."

"Oh, that often happens. The spouse kicks off and then the one who's left behind goes too. When did his wife die?"

Marina looked down at the article, "1968," she said.

The sky had blackened up and was preparing to unleash a storm. In a few moments we would begin to hear rain tap on the windows and hammer into the deck like Japanese nails.

"Some women want me to coach their soccer team," I said.

"Do it," Marina responded, "You need an outside activity. The suburbs are death's heart beating slowly in green chambers, and it's not as if you have anything else to do."

"I thought you liked it here," I said.

Marina bit into her plum; a skein of purple skin lodged above her upper lip and turned her for a moment into Frida Kahlo. Then the rain came. A solitary tear rolled slowly down her cheek.

"The children are almost grown," she said.

"I'm not going to do it," I replied. "I love the game of soccer too much."

"You're a snob and a misogynist," Marina replied.

"There are worse things to be," I replied.

On account of faux-death and unemployment pounding on my jaw and demanding entrance I couldn't coach anyway. Instead, I was in Boston's famous Brigham and Women's Hospital, where a century ago, the pregnant Brahmins and dowagers of Beacon Hill lay in waiting to greet their off-spring. I had been admitted overnight because a tumor, rumoured to be benign, had attached to a long hidden wisdom tooth and needed to be stolen from a dark recess of my jaw. I had a morphine pump that I could activate every seven minutes, and access, via a huge remote, to a basic cable package. The remote also moved the bed up and down. The guy in the next bed, Jack, looked like a recent arrestee from "Cops." He had a full body tattoo, streaked blond hair, and an interesting way with words His arm was bandaged from hand to elbow. While performing some slippery roofing he had accidentally almost severed two of his fingers with a chain saw. At the local hospital on Cape Cod they thought full amputation might be the way to go but at the Brigham they got out the needle and thread and went to work. Now he was on the phone to his fiancée Martha "I'm in a fucking WOMEN'S hospital," he yelled, "Don't tell anyone." At 5:15am my PCP Dr Morton Apfelbaum came in to pay me one of his predawn visits. He has done this to me before, sneaking in like the ghost that visits Ivan Karamazov, and set-tling with folded feathers, by the side of my bed.

"What's with the fucking bow tie?" my inquisitive room-mate wanted to know. Morton ignored him. My TV was switched off but Jack had a Jerry Springer re-run going full blast. "Fucking homos," he said. I thought, in my morphine haze, that he might have been referring to Morton and myself (the bow tie?) but in fact he was talking to the TV.

"What," Morton asked, "is a compound odontoma?"

It was strange that he had chosen this moment to test me on medical arcana. After all, he could see that I was in trouble.

"I give up," I murmured. I was floating on a wide brown river.

"That was your condition. That is what necessitated your surgery."

"Get your fat fucking ass down here right now," my roommate said. He was holding the phone in his good hand and sending a message to Martha. "Fucking doctors! Fucking nurses. I haven't slept for twelve days and as soon as I fall asleep they wake me up. And you know what they give me?"

Martha didn't know.

"Eggs. Scrambled eggs. Can you believe that shit?"

My surgeon, Norm Roberts, swept in. He had played strong safety for Cornell but twenty years on, the muscle had turned to fat. Lately, it seemed, he had grown obsessed with *Napoleon Dynamite* which was, along with *Dodgeball*, one of his two favorite films.

"Gosh," he said (as Napoleon) "*TEEnaa* eat it." Then he went back to Norm and laughed, "Except you can't eat anything," he continued, "not for 48 hours, until the swelling has subsided."

"Hi Norm," Morton said from under his invisible cloak.

Shortly after my release I ran into my ex-masseuse Rochelle Shavinsky in the car park of our local Whole Foods Store. She jumped out of a sparkling green Lexus SUV whose colour matched her eyes. She was in the local uniform for athletic women her age, sweatpants and zip-top but she had carried something sexy from Baku that transcended the outfit. Or maybe it was simply that the zip was halfway down her breasts. She almost walked right past me, but then decided to stop.

"So," she said, "You won't coach. You are a pig and a coward."

"I didn't know you were on the team."

"Would that have made a difference?"

"Maybe," I lied, which is something that expanded cleavage can make you do.

"I can't be on the team, I'm not in shape."

"You look in shape to me."

"What would you know? You eat too much and you don't exercise."

Both these things were true. My jaw began to throb and my right cheek felt like Squirrel Nutkin's.

"What's the team called anyway?"

"Ellen did not tell you? *The Furies,* they are called *The Furies.*"

"Didn't they rip men to pieces?"

"Exactly."

Rochelle sprang off to buy orange juice, or perhaps it was a heat-seeking missile that she was after.

Women's soccer was total crap. Everybody knew it and nobody would say it. All those ridiculous ad campaigns comparing Mia Hamm to Pele; in the true American man's arena of football, hockey, basketball and baseball such absurdist hyperbole would not be countenanced.

I had six months severance pay coming and all the weeks of an unusually disappointing Fall — no russet reds, no vivid yellow — in which to find a job. All around me the sweet birds sang "Relent, relent." I decided to forgo a late Sunday afternoon rerun of *Rome* "GastroEnteritis! Caesar's legions are massing by the river!" and head down to the muddy soccer fields at Cold Spring Park. The wan October sun rolled out of the clouds and slid its pale lemon light between the maple and oak trees that loomed behind the goalposts. And here were the women, The Furies, who called to one another and kicked a spinning orb — a ball? A man's head? — like the angry ones of old.

When I found her Ellen Brody was sitting on the touchline wrapping her left ankle.

"Hi," I said, "I'm JJ."

"Wawaweewa," she said, pretending to be Borat from the Ali G. Show. "Am I supposed to get excited about that?"

"I've changed my mind. I'd like to coach. I'd *love* to coach."

I pointed at my vaguely swollen cheek as if, somehow, that explained everything.

"You want me to kiss you?" Ellen asked.

"My tooth," I replied, "I had a compound odontoma. That's why I never got back to you."

Ellen took a deep breath.

"It's too late," she said, "we found someone else."

And then I saw Adonis, his gold curls tinged bronze by the October sun, approaching in a halo of leaves across the field. It really was Adonis, the Greek hairdresser from Needham Street, and not the god. We had once played together on an Over 30's team and he had taught me how to say "Son of a Whore" and "Bastard" in the language of Salonika.

"Hey," Adonis shouted above the din, "what are you doing here?"

In the distance the park worker cut off his leaf blower.

"Nothing," I replied.

"OK, ladies," Adonis said, "Let's get cracking."

The women lined up. Adonis had them all do some stretching followed by a light jog around the pitch. While they were gone he walked over to me.

"My brother Fotis was in Iraq," he said, "he got shot in the shoulder. Now he's home. He was lucky."

We watched the women in two's and single file as they slow-paced through the encroaching smoky dusk. Every so often one of them would rise to head an imaginary ball, her hair flapping luxurious in the wind. I didn't know what to say about Fotis Lysandrou, so I said nothing.

"Are you still playing?" Adonis asked.

"No," I replied, "I packed it in. My knees gave up on me."

"I'm done too. Pacemaker."

"Jesus."

"I know. What can you do?"

I walked home via the aqueduct. Everything that was good and sporting and hopeful and innocent, like women's soccer, suddenly seemed especially sweet to me. On the front lawn of our house Marina was raking leaves.

"Now it is autumn," she said, "And the falling leaves. And the long journey towards oblivion."

Early the next morning I called Adonis at his place of work. It sounded as if he had eight hairdryers going at once.

"Can I be your assistant?" I asked.

"What?" he yelled.

I repeated my question.

"For the soccer or for the hairdressing?"

"Both," I replied.

Blum's Daughters
Zvi Jagendorf

Die Lotte and Mr Blum were stirring things up on the beach. There was no doubt about that. She would sit in the deck chair and flaunt her legs at him, bony but smooth and well oiled. She stretched a lot in that chair and shifted about on the canvas like a slippery fish on a plate. Mr Blum watched her in his shirtsleeves, with his hat on. He used to wear a suit even when he came to the beach, usually brown like his hat and his pockets bulged with newspapers. Mr Blum didn't have a wife. She was dead *over there* somewhere but he had two daughters Gerda and Paula who had interesting breasts and frizzy hair and were older than me and Spitz but not much.

"She's wriggling for him," said Spitz as we watched them from our forward observation post near the ice cream stand. "She's doing the rhumba sitting down so that he'll have it etched on his brain when he goes back to London to make more money."

"D'you really think they do it?" I said.

I couldn't imagine Lotte actually letting any man touch her, never mind lying *on* her. She looked nylon-wrapped and lacquered like a trophy in a glass cupboard. Spitz was less certain, after all he didn't think he was Shulim's son.

"Glumfy is not my dad, any idiot can see that. He's dark and he's got a moonface. I'm bloody well blond and my chin

113

comes to the point of a perfect triangle with my blue eyes. Anyway I can see by the way he looks at me. He's not my father, never was."

According to Spitz his mother had been the mistress of a big doctor in Vienna and kept seeing him even after she was married off to Shulim Perl and his family business. Spitz worked this out from the obsessive way Lotte talked about the great doctors she knew over there and how they made a woman feel so taken care of. She didn't say things like this to us but we heard her babbling in her endless chats with Gina Holtz on the phone.

"Yes und they were so *fein*, immediately they knew why my cheeks were flushing. There was another kind of people. More civilised."

Spitz believed the worst of his mother just as she believed the worst about him.

"Bet she told my so called dad, 'Just off for a little checkup, *mein schatz*. One of my regular little medical checkups, you know.'"

He spent hours inspecting the brown envelopes stuffed with little photographs they had brought from Vienna. He tried to get her to identify all the young people in bathing suits sitting by a lake somewhere, or the young man in a sombrero twirling her round at some dance.

"You don't have to know all these things," she'd say, "better you spend time doing your homework."

So she was hiding something. It was obvious.

As for Shulim, he never came to the seaside. He kept quiet, mooned around, went to work and prayed a lot wrapped up in his *tallis* early in the morning when the house was quiet. You could hear him clear enough like a big heavy animal singing or a whale mourning the loss of its mate. So he wasn't with us at Mrs Blake's *Traditional Vegetarian Bed and*

Breakfast and we went to the seaside with Gerda and Paula whose father, Blum, booked them into a classy hotel with a swimming pool and a band. The girls spent the days with us and he visited when he felt like looking at Lotte's legs and oiled up tummy.

Blum owned houses in London and people paid him rent to live in bits of them. He was a mysterious man who didn't even live in England all the time but turned up suddenly after a short phone call from Brussels or New York or even Brazzaville. He had put his girls in a fancy boarding school and part of Lotte's job was to show a motherly interest in them. The other part was to collect rent and put it in Blum's account. That was all. Perhaps it was.

Lotte was getting ready to go in the water. For this she had to pull on her bathing cap and recomb the bit of hair she left outside for effect. Then she had to put on a few new kinds of cream and stretch her crumpled bathing suit across her thin rump while Blum feasted his eyes.

The evening before she had taken us for a walk along the sea front making us all link arms, Gerda, Paula, Spitz, me and she while she sang *"Ein Spanischer tango und ein madchen wie du,"* traipsing along past the seafront junk stands and doing dance steps for everyone to see. Gerda and Paula quite liked it, you could tell they enjoyed being looked at, but Spitz dropped hands and pretended he wasn't with this crowd of jerks singing in German.

"Come on. Come on," Lotte shouted. She waved her arms like a flamenco dancer and her breasts jiggled inside her sweater. She grabbed hold of Gerda's waist and did this weird dance pressed together, stopping and starting while she sang till she got red in the face.

"Well done ladies," said one of the onlookers and a few of them actually clapped. Spitz was cursing energetically and practically spitting down my neck. Nothing his mother did pleased him, not when she was serious and practical and not when she was in a bubbly mood. The frosty jailer in a house-coat pushing him out of bed on a cold morning was no better than the flirt skipping along the sea front in white bell bottoms and a red sweater. She was his mother therefore she could do no right.

The way Blum was looking at her she could do no wrong. He was shielding his eyes with the *Daily Express* and following her every move as she made her way down to the water. She had quite a nice shape though she stooped a bit as if she was afraid of taking full responsibility for her uncovered body. On the pictures from the Vienna Woods she didn't look at all shy. In one of them she had her hands on her hips in a really cheeky pose: come and get me, *schatz*. Soon we lost sight of her except for the blue ball of her bathing cap bobbing along in the green sea. Blum sank back in his deck chair and Gerda and Paula appeared red and sweaty from their tennis practice.

They soon figured out where we were in our observation post and marched over. They were quite big girls, good wrestlers and slippery twisters when it came to running with a ball.

"All the nice girls love a racket. All the bad girls love a ball," sang Spitz. He pretended to make fun of their tennis but it was very soft fun for a viper like him. These were girls who were like family and strangers at the same time. They smelled good and had smooth skin and special manners but their father was like our lot, a messy old bear who spoke odd English and almost never took off his hat.

"Let's go and swim at the hotel," said Gerda, "we can dive there and no flies thank you."

We were up in a second and we all bounded along the path from the beach not saying much but connected in some way to each other. I walked behind Paula and saw her ankles riding neatly in her sandal straps like fresh shoots sprouting in a garden. I was dying to touch them but I would have had to tackle her from behind and we weren't playing wrestle ball at the time, so I had to just think about it. Spitz and Gerda were walking side by side and it seemed there was no space between them at all, just his and her shoulders keeping time together. I was really happy in that short walk. I forgot everything except the fun of us four being together. It was like floating in a lovely thin bubble connected to nothing but the sunlight.

The pool was quite cold and Spitz showed off his commando crawl, though the girls swam faster and splashed less. Their school obviously had fancy gym and sports teachers who knew what they were doing, not like the sadistic ex-soldiers who pushed us about at our penal colony.

Afterwards when we were drying off Gerda said something odd to Spitz:

"Do your mother and your dad sleep in the same bed?"

I wasn't listening all that closely at first because Paula was lying on her towel quite close to me and I could see the goose pimples on her arms and the little drops of water coming off her hair. But she repeated her question when Spitz didn't answer.

"Do your mother and your dad sleep in the same bed?"

That was one even Spitz couldn't have foreseen. He rolled over and squinted at the pool.

"They sleep in the same room."

She wouldn't budge. She wasn't letting go of the bone.

"In one bed?"

"Sort of."

"What does that mean?

"Two beds parallel with a space between them equaling

the sum of the circumference of the triangle formed by feet, hot water bottle and pillows divided by three."

"Couples who don't share one bed are stuck in an anti-sexual marriage" said Gerda loud and clear.

Spitz didn't like that coming from her. He could have said much worse about Lotte and Shulim any time but to hear it from this girl in posh English with all the wisdom of the boarding school dorm made him angry.

"What d'you know about couples. Your mum is dead."

Spitz was a cruel talker but he usually kept off the subject of dead parents. That was a minefield.

"Yes, but when she was alive they had a sexual marriage."

"How do you know?"

"I saw pictures."

"Of what? Your father snogging with your mother?"

As soon as he said it he was sorry he had. I could see that by the way he pushed his face in the towel and tensed up his neck. Paula next to me pretended she wasn't listening but she was. Her eyes were closed in that false fluttering way. Should I touch her shoulder, I wondered, as if to brush off the last drops of water or as if to show I knew all about dead mothers? Her face was really close and it seemed like the face of an orphan girl waiting for a mother's kiss.

Gerda was quiet for a bit but she was just planning her move. She and Spitz were quite alike except she was daring and he was reckless and angry.

"You make them sound like animals. But they're just people. Is kissing 'snogging'? You've probably never seen people really in love. If you had you'd know it from a picture."

Gerda could have been Deborah Kerr then if it hadn't been for the tangled black wire of her hair and the bouncy mouth. She was already half way out of our prison. She was over the wall of that dreary world of brown rooms and jittery parents with their naturalisation papers and lists of dead relatives. She was going to be free, I could tell. I mean her father had probably left her mother behind *over there* for some good reason that we could never understand and here was Gerda with a picture of a couple of young people in a park or getting on a train to Italy and she was full of hope about them. They were in love. Never mind that one of them was going to disappear and the other had turned into Mr Blum in the brown hat sitting on the beach with an eyeful of Lotte and a pocketful of newspapers.

I felt sorry for Paula and I touched her shoulder near where it joins up with the neck. That's a really pretty spot on girls; it's sort of secret but not too much and it isn't forbidden or dangerous. She let me stay there and we both listened, happy to be out of it. I thought I felt her blood flowing bringing that good flush to her face and keeping her toes well arranged and snug in a curvy row.

"Married couples don't make love," said Spitz, getting up to fight another round, "they procreate and haggle. 'Yes, no, oo ah, now, stopit, close the window, turn the tap off.' It's worse than penal servitude." He was watching Gerda hungrily as if he would turn into a vulture if she showed any sign of weakness and tear her flesh off her bones in long strips.

Gerda answered by pushing him hard on his chest with both hands and trying to pin him down. She was heavier but he was elastic and turned the tables on her in no time. Now she was under him his brown hands held down her shoulders.

"Say 'procreate and haggle' ten times and I'll let you go."

"Never, you broomstick."

"Say it under your breath."

"It under your breath."

"Say I give in."

"Say you give in."

They were practically nose to nose. It was as like a kiss as anything and it meant no losers no winners, until the next time. Spitz and Gerda lay still next to each other. They had put a lot into that fight and their exhaustion spread over the four of us like a fog over a little dinghy at sea.

"Gerda, Paula," through the mist in my head I heard their names called. Blum was looking for his daughters. The brown bear in the hat was barreling down the path to the pool waving his newspaper and trumpeting their names through his nose. "Gerduuuh Pauluuuhhh." Soon he was standing between us and the sun smelling of tobacco and eau de cologne.

"Come, girls and boys, how about a trip, all of us together? It will be fun for sure."

The girls were up in a second. They loved their pa and didn't get to see him much so any trip was a treat. It was pretty to watch how they draped themselves all over him, sort of hanging from his neck and shoulders like baby jaguars he had caught on a hunting expedition. But Spitz and I both resented his marching in on us like Napoleon rallying the troops and taking charge of the girls we thought were only with us.

We trailed back to the beach behind them in a foul mood because they seemed to have forgotten we were even there. "O Daddy this" and "O Daddy that," and squeals and giggles. They seemed to shrink back into kids as he sucked the woman out of them. I looked down at my knees. They were bright red, burnt and already tingling.

Lotte was dressed and made up, ready to have fun in her orange and yellow beach suit and big white hat. She looked like a tropical plant in Kew Gardens, brash, waxy and fragile at the same time.

"So we take a boat to Bell Island?" she said.

Blum looked hesitant. He probably had a bus ride in mind to a place where you could eat. But the girls loved the idea of the rocky bird sanctuary out in the bay. So Bell Island it had to be.

In the boat Lotte couldn't stop talking about the trips she and all her pals took out of Vienna, "in the beeeuutiful zommer, you know." We chopped along in the breeze with the other trippers and she wasn't paying any attention to the beach or the pier slipping away behind us. She was back in her teens, taking walks in the mountains with Emil and Piroshka and the handsome, nameless son of the famous architect who always turned up in her stories. If you believed her they drank milk hot off the cow, ate fresh berries, heard far away echoes of bells from deep valleys and lay in the sweet grass looking into the sky for hours and hours. Emil was going to be a doctor " but you know what happened to him." She said this automatically, without stopping or taking a breath. It was like Emil's surname: Mr. Emil *Youknowhathappenedtohim* M.D. (almost). Blum wasn't really listening. He seemed caught in the net of his daughters' arms. They had him tied up between them, nestling close and letting him shield them from the spray. Lotte's words flew over him and scattered in the breeze and as Spitz never listened to her on principle I was the one whose job it was to nod and make eye contact. Her stories didn't bore me in spite of Spitz's's contempt because my mother might have been one of those young people out on a Viennese picnic and I never got to hear her story.

On the island Mr Blum and Lotte looked really odd, him in his suit and hat, her in screaming colours. It was bare and blown clean by the wind so they stood out like a pair of carnival puppets against the sky. The other trippers went off with binoculars to look for birds and plants but we had no plans and no food either. We started climbing up away from the jetty and pretty soon we might have been alone on a rock in the middle of the ocean. Even Lotte quietened down and put her hat away letting the wind do what it liked with her hair. I wondered what would happen if we had to spend the rest of our lives on this island. How long would it take before we began to hate each other and worse? Would we all lose our shame and would Blum take off his hat? How could I ever hate Paula? She could easily hate me though with my ridiculous burnt knees and Spitz could hate anybody anywhere. I looked at us all and saw us naked and screaming at each other like seagulls fighting over fish.

"Stop here and I'll take a nice picture," said Lotte mining her bag for the camera. Blum moved his papers from one pocket to the other and cleared his throat. He even made a move towards his neck to tighten the knot of his non-existent tie. The girls arranged themselves at his feet and Spitz and I hung about on the edge of the group. Lottie clicked and held out the camera to me.

"Come on. You take one of me as well."

Blum put out a gallant hand to show her where to stand, next to him. She sailed into the space and moved as close to him as she could. She didn't put her hands on her hips like in the "come and get me *schatz*" photograph. They seemed not to know where to go. Her face was cheeky and tilted but her hands just hung there like limp rope. I suppose she was afraid to put them where they wanted to be, on the body of the man next to her.

"This we make big," she said, "and frame it."

There wasn't much soft earth of any kind on the island but we found a hollow of sorts and left Lotte and Blum there while we went off to explore. I gave Paula my hand to pull her up over a rock and kept it there. What I touched was warm and quite small but it was big enough to block out any other sensation. I might have been in a cave in total darkness with only this touch to tell me I was alive and not a bat.

Gerda and Spitz climbed away fast and soon all we could hear was an occasional shout of laughter or of protest from their direction. They were probably arguing like mad and you know what *that* leads to.

Paula was quiet but it was the kind of quiet that says: listen to all the words I am saying in my head and you will know. So I thought the best thing to do was to stay quiet as well and get her curious.

"What are you so *shtum* for?" she said.

I was amazed but I didn't show it. It was like a secret password between us, a word we heard at home and nowhere else.

"I'm listening."

"To what?"

"To what you're not saying."

"What am I not saying?"

"You're not saying what you're thinking."

"OK, you tell me and I'll tell you?"

Clever little fox. She had nailed me. I took a dive.

"I'll tell you what you're thinking. Then you tell me what I'm thinking."

She laughed. She liked the danger of that.

"You," I said, "you..." I was attacked by a million thoughts like pieces of shattered glass flying through the air. None of them had any shape.

"You're bored by this holiday. You wish you could go somewhere glamorous."

She looked at me full faced with two green eyes targeting my hot forehead. There was nowhere to hide.

"You," she said, "are scared of me. You put thoughts like

that into my head because you are running away. That's a real joke 'glamorous'. What's in it for you to have me out of here? Where would I go?"

For a second I thought she was going to cry. But she was just angry. So I went on.

"With your friends from school to the Norfolk Broads." I didn't know where on earth the Norfolk Broads were but I knew that people totally unlike Shulim, Lotte and the rest of us went there in boats and had drinks at country inns.

Paula was laughing, shaking her head at the craziness of it. She folded her hands behind her and did a mocking strut around me.

"Oh mai deah, we must take ah beoat out on the Brahds. Doo come along and bring your papa, dear old Blum."

She lay down on the hard earth and looked straight up at the sky. Her lips were dry and chapped by the wind. I sat down next to her and put my hand on her mouth. She gave it a real, controlled bite but I didn't pull away. It was as if I had been expecting it. I just pressed a little harder on her lips and felt her tongue and teeth nestling inside. There was nothing separating us, just some air and light, so I kissed her and she kissed me back. She tasted of salt and cinnamon.

We lay there eye to eye, nose to nose, forehead to forehead and I touched her hair which felt rough and wiry to my fingers. I didn't know where to put my hands so I just held her as best as I could which wasn't as good as the quiet touch on the nape of her neck at the pool. It's better when the girl isn't facing you. That's odd when you come to think of it. She closed her eyes a bit but most of the time in between kisses she was looking at me from quite close.

Her eye seemed huge and naked, bigger than my whole face.

"Look at me," she said, "look me in the eyes."

She could have been a hypnotist because she pulled me hard without any pressure of her arms. Her green eyes did it all. They practically swallowed me. If it hadn't been for my burning knees I could have blacked out. But the itch was getting unbearable and I couldn't pretend any more. So I sat up and hugged my knees.

"They're roasted," she said," poor thing."

"Who killed Cock Robin?"

"What?"

"Poor thing he's dead, his knees went crimson red."

Paula too was getting away. I could hear it by the way she said "poor thing," imitating her games mistress's cool sympathy.

Poor Blum. I was sorry for him. He would never be able to talk like that and keep up with his daughters. His suit and hat were going to be an embarrassment. "That's my father, Blum." "Poor thing, where does he get his clothes, at the pawnbrokers?" "And where's your mother?" "*Over there.* Somewhere."

She touched me from behind and put her hands on my shoulders.

"You're nice," she said, "nice and moody and you're thinking bad thoughts about me."

"Never."

"I just kissed you and you hate me."

I kept still.

"I'll guess why. Because you think I'll kiss anyone. Because I'm a bit older than you. Because I go to a fancy school. Because my name is Paula and I'm not sorry enough for myself."

I wondered how serious she was. Her voice had no mockery in it but I didn't know. I turned round and her face was taut and sad. I wondered if she missed her mother at all, but

I couldn't ask her. She looked frail yet I didn't know how to protect her or comfort her or even keep her near me.

"I'm sorry," I said, "I don't know how to have fun. But I don't hate you. I like you. I like you a lot. I just keep thinking."

"What?"

"That you'll disappear and I'll never see you again."

"But we come on holiday with you and Lotte every year."

I felt the tears breaking out of their bags and speeding towards my eyes. But just then pebbles started raining down on us from the hill.

"Repent, miserable sinners. Confess. The end is near."

Gerda and Spitz, flushed and rowdy, came slithering down, holding onto each other like a couple of drunks.

Spitz gave us a quick look over. He decided to ignore what he saw.

"We'd better go and see what the fathers and mothers are doing, before it's too late."

We scrambled back to where we had left them. The girls were talking very loud, practically screeching. They were trying to make sure we didn't surprise their dad, I thought. They don't want to be embarrassed. But when we got to the place Blum was alone. He was lying on some newspapers with his jacket off and his shirt unbuttoned as far as his belt. His hat was lying there, upended, rejected and useless like a leaky boat. He seemed to be asleep, red faced and breathing loudly through his nose. The crinkly hairs on his chest grew thickly almost up to his neck yet he had smooth cheeks. Where was Lotte? There was no sign of her though her beach bag, various bottles of cream, her floppy hat and orange jacket were strewn around the area. We stood above the hollow like police at the scene of a crime. There's a queer feeling you have when you watch parents asleep; you imagine them dead and you are cold and distant from those big bodies wrapped around their organs and veins and arteries. There's nothing you can tell them anymore. You're on your own.

"Yoo hoo, yoo hoo."

Lotte, bare shouldered and sunburned, was waving at us from the path leading down to the sea. She zigzagged up towards us, swaying a bit and stumbling on the uneven ground. Her face was quite red and sweat had dissolved her mascara giving her sooty rings around her eyes. She looked like a fireman back from a blaze.

"He wasn't feeling so good, a stomach ache," she said, "so I went to see if you can get a cup of tea here. We should have brought some food."

The girls were down by Blum's side in an instant, fussing over him, buttoning his shirt and wiping the sweat off his face. He seemed distant but alright and he let them flutter about without saying much. He didn't look at Lotte, I saw that.

She watched them hungrily muttering half sarcastically, "such good girls, taking care of their father, such nice girls." Spitz nudged me with his elbow. Lotte's praise was always a mask for envy. There was only so much "taking care" to be had in the world and she who took care of Blum's girls for him wasn't getting any for herself while he was getting more than his fair share right before our eyes.

He was on his feet now, jacket back on, hat in place and he looked the old Blum, crumpled and a bit shifty, or mysterious if you were being nice. I suppose he had women in the places he travelled to. Black women in Africa, white women in America. Lotte was too much like home-cooking for him, probably. Perhaps she reminded him of when he was a young man in Vienna and that's why he stared at her so much. They might have known each other *over there* even though they didn't talk about it in front of us. She could have been a friend of Gerda and Paula's mother. If that was true he was probably wondering if the girl he married would have turned into Lotte Perl the Second.

On the way back he was too polite to her, practically wiping the seat on the boat with his handkerchief and listening intently to her blabber but looking solidly out to sea through his glasses. Gerda and Spitz were deep in conversation with some birdwatchers. They were leading them on pretending they were Swedish hikers, doing the accents and picking up each other's lies like a couple of sharks in a kiddy pool.

I stood behind Paula at the rail and felt the heat of the long morning in her shoulders. Blum and Lotte were laughing at something, I think I heard them talking Yiddish or German. Paula put her hand in mine. As the pier drew near I realised I was very hungry and that another holiday together, perhaps the last, was nearly over.

The Reservoir Room
Tamar Yellin

High in the hills she found the reservoir room. A small round
room like a folly, with a domed roof topped by a lightning
rod, twelve tall windows and a tall door. A room surrounded
by water, reached only by a slim footbridge.

She wanted it. But it was the property of the Water
Authority. It housed the sluice engine for the reservoir. At
first the Water Authority would not budge on the matter.
Finally she persuaded them to accept a generous rent.

The big sluice engine filled the middle of the room. The
round walls could not accommodate much furniture. She had
some items specially designed: a curved table to sit at and a
curved bed, on which she lay in a crescent position.

At first she could not sleep for the sound of lapping water.
But she soon got used to it, and before long she did not know
how she had ever tolerated square and waterless rooms.

She hung no curtains at her twelve windows. Every morning she awoke at dawn. Light reflected from the water and
moved in vivid patches on the floor and ceiling, on the white
bed and on her own body. Sometimes, her face touched by a
finger of moonlight, she woke to a reservoir full of broken
stars.

She sat and watched the world from her twelve windows.
And being exceptionally keen-eyed she saw a number of

things: lovers lying under haystacks, lovers lying under trees; the mole-catcher laying poison with his gloved hands. Once there was a heron, once there was a fox. Geese came skimming over the water with their wings ajar.

She sat at her twelve windows and watched the world. And with the eyes of her imagination she saw lovers lying under minarets, lovers lying under domes; ex-lovers strewing poison on a dish of dates. Once there was a tiger, once there was a snake. Fish went flying over the African sea.

Day after day she sat at her twelve windows. This was all she had ever wanted: to watch the world. Not to be disturbed or interrupted. Not to talk or take part. Now at last she had found the place to do it. She had been looking all her life for the reservoir room.

★★★

The villagers were not happy about the occupant of the reservoir sluice room.

They had not been consulted. And they thought it strange. Why should anyone choose to live there? Surely it was unhygienic.

Nevertheless they were prepared to be friendly. When they met her coming up the hill from the reservoir they smiled and said hello. She never responded, she never smiled. Bob Robbins, the landlord of *The Packhorse*, had caught her emptying her chemical toilet in the ladies' loo.

A bit strange in the head, then, was she? Well, there were plenty of those! But she had no curtains at her windows. They saw her all the time, sitting, sitting, and then, at other times, in various states of undress. Someone should call a policeman. As for the ladies, they wouldn't dream of looking, but the men felt it their duty to check up on her occasionally through a pair of shared binoculars.

Sometimes she bought pilchards in the village shop. She never said please or thank you: she pointed to what she required. Elsie Flannery had been unable to interest her in a copy of the village newsletter, *Folk*. Was she a deaf-mute, perhaps? No, she had been heard muttering to herself. The Reverend Briggs had gone down to the sluice room, but she wouldn't open.

They would have liked to help. Provide blankets, perhaps, or a transistor radio. Wasn't she terribly lonely in that place? They questioned each other, shrugged their shoulders, shook their heads. But there were no answers. It was inexplicable.

★★★

Her solitude was not entirely uninterrupted. Every so often the equipment needed to be operated or inspected, and a maintenance worker was sent by the Water Authority, who retained an absolute right of access and also possessed the key.

It was not possible to warn her of these visits. He arrived unannounced, and with the courtesy of a brief knock would burst in at any hour of the day or night. He wore blue overalls with the logo of the Water Authority, he smelt of sweat and petrol and carried, always, an enormous torch.

"How're you liking it, then?" he would ask, grinning. And he turned the giant stopcock with his callused hands. Then he would add: "Darn funny place to want to live, in my opinion."

She stood watching him, and it sometimes seemed to her that if he turned the stopcock far enough, the room and all its windows and the two of them would sink slowly down beneath the reservoir.

She appealed to the Water Authority. She could supervise the machinery herself. The Water Authority would not hear of it. They could not have their equipment tampered with by unlicensed personnel. Any damage would result in the immediate termination of her tenancy.

So she was forced to admit the man. She never spoke to him, but he didn't seem to notice. He carried on a continuous conversation with himself. "So where are you from?" he would ask. "Don't tell me: it's obvious. Running away from something? Aren't we all, my darling, aren't we all. Now this valve, that's the blighter. And this gauge," he tapped it, "that's the one to watch." When he had gone the room felt strangely restless. She had to walk round and round to calm herself.

And the villagers, watching from their back windows through binoculars, saw the crazy woman walking round and round. They had grown used to her now, they almost took her for granted. She was the subject of a feature article and many humorous references in their monthly newsletter, *Folk*.

It took her a long time to recover from the man's visits. But eventually she grew calm again and sat in her accustomed seat. She looked through the narrow tablet of her seventh window with such intensity they wondered what she saw. They thought perhaps that she was staring at them. But while they could see only her, she could see anything she wanted; and not all her visions were delightful ones.

★★★

Autumn came. From her twelve windows she watched the leaves turn in the woods of the world, and the lovers who had lain in the corn all summer rise and separate. Then it turned colder. Snow fell; a hard wind blew across the water and the grey waves stiffened against the walls of the reservoir room.

The villagers worried about her. Wasn't it freezing in there? Then they ceased to worry. It was her choice, after all. She had refused their hospitality when it was offered. It was not their business, now, to interfere.

The man from the Water Authority was disquieted. When he entered the room he could see his own breath. He tried to coax her, question her. She would not answer. He began to offer her things. She accepted a sheepskin, a magenta blanket. He stopped by with a paraffin stove.

He said: "Why don't you jack it in, all this? It's no good in winter. Find yourself a proper place for the duration. You can always come back again in spring."

She seemed to listen. Her look was contemptuous, but she said nothing.

"What's it about anyway," he said, "you living here? Some kind of a demonstration? Believe me, sweetheart, nobody's interested."

He leaned forward and added confidentially: "Do yourself a favour. Put some curtains up."

***

She was devastated. The next day she ordered thirty-six metres of blackout material.

She fixed up blackouts at each of the twelve windows. But she could not be natural, she could not be content. Wasn't there a crack there, where a line of light appeared? Couldn't they see through, was the fabric thick enough? She sat behind the blackouts, rigid in her chair, and felt the eyes of telescopes and periscopes and all the binoculars of the world focusing on her.

She looked at each of her windows in turn. The first was blank; the second and third showed only blankness. The fourth and fifth were empty, the sixth and seventh also void. Shouldn't the imagination be limitless? In dreams she had seen some astonishing things, and she closed her eyes now, but she could summon nothing out of the dark.

And the villagers trained their binoculars on the reservoir

sluice room, and were amazed, frustrated; they could not believe the stranger's effrontery. How dared she presume their interest in her? And what was she up to now behind those screens? The Water Authority would be angry, the Water Authority must be informed. Their property was being exploited for unlikely practices.

The man from the Water Authority said, sadly: "I only meant her to put up *net* curtains." But it was too late. She would have nothing to do with him. From now on, whenever he entered the room, she left it.

★★★

The cold was intense. Leaves and ferns of frost formed on the windows of the reservoir room.

The whole world was hidden, and she was hidden from the world. She was filled with an enormous boredom. She lay down on her curved white bed and fell asleep.

She did not know how many days she lay there motionless. And this was her vision: one morning she awoke and knew that she was not alone. On the contrary, the room was full of people. Faces gazed at her from every side.

In sudden terror she jumped up and rushed away from them. The others rushed away like the opening petals of a flower.

She remained still, and the rest too were still as though patiently waiting. She moved towards one, and all moved forward with a simultaneous tread.

Then she realised that they were not strangers.

She put out a hand, and touched her own image in the silvered glass.

★★★

134

The villagers heard the noise of a disturbance. The sound of breaking windows was coming from the reservoir sluice room.

By the time they reached it, through the snow, everything was quiet. But the lock was frozen. They couldn't get in.

"Whatever's happened," muttered Elsie Flannery, "it's her own fault."

"She brought it on herself," Bob Robbins had to agree. For neither approved of people who took things to extremes.

The man from the Water Authority told them they were trespassing. They drew back and waited on the roadside while he fetched his tools.

The crowbar was not enough, and they brought mattocks and a battering ram. It took three people to break down the door of the reservoir room.

A gust of cold air met them, and the room was covered in a light dusting of snow. There was no-one there. In place of the twelve windows were twelve broken mirrors.

The Love that Comes from Saving Their Lives

Shaun Levin

Thelma's telling them the story for the thousandth time.

She says: "And then in the end..." she says, "When the train got to Lesotho there were banana trees all over the place."

I can tell by her voice that she's stretching her arms out to the sides, like she's showing them what the whole world looks like. She tells the two little ones again and again about those bunches of bananas and the high banana trees. She tells them like it's the end of the story and that's all that matters. Poor girl, she wants them to think it all worked out fine in the end. Children like stories with happy endings. I see it all the time in the little ones. They like to listen to stories they've heard before, to have them told over and over again.

I just keep my eyes shut because I know what she's going to say. I feel her looking at me sitting here in the chair, pretending to be fast asleep. Then she says: "You see, it was Granny who saved us all in the end."

The children giggle away. Each time they hear the story, they laugh, their tiny little minds trying to digest Thelma's story, trying to match it up with this wrinkled old granny who makes fudge and wears funny clothes and takes them to see the dolphins on Saturday morning.

"How can Granny save you?" the little one says.

"Oh, but she did," Thelma says.

"Did Grampa help her?"

Thelma knows I'm wide awake and that's why she says all this. For my own sake and for the children's.

"Oh, no," she says. "Granny did it all on her own."

But I know she hates me. She hates me for taking her so far from home. Did I have a choice? Have I ever had a choice? What does she know how it was for me? It was lovely for them. It was. For the two of them it was fantastic. For Thelma and David it was wonderful, they were safe and warm. Not all the blankets we needed, not as much food as we would have liked, but we got out of there in time, in one piece. And once we made it to this place it was all perfect. They were happy. And why not? It's paradise.

Only later did Mr Bruno make his entrance. Back from the dead. I said to myself: Esther Rivka, don't even bother with the questions. *Schemzich*. You don't want to know and you don't need to know. There he came, their father, in his long socks and safari suit, marching through the jungle like a Mr Livingstone, smiling away. All I could think was: You *nebech*, don't come showing me that *verkakte* face? Why would anyone want to see you? But then I said to myself: where else in the world does he have to go?

They went to the convent, the two of them. It makes me laugh. If you think what happened with that woman of his and everything. Jewish children, my children, ending up there in a school full of *goyim* and Jesus nailed to the wall above the blackboard. But did I have a choice? No choice, no nothing. That's the story of my life. No choices. All you can do is make choices for other people.

"Mommy, can we go now," the little one says. She's five. The boy, Thomas, is seven. It's his birthday. We're going to The

Ranch for burgers.

"As soon as Daddy gets back from work," Thelma says.

"And what about Granny?" Thomas says. "Granny's still sleeping."

"Shh," Thelma says. "Let her sleep. Granny's tired."

And what happens? Gerda from the post office comes running with the telex like somebody had died, God forbid. Bruno was doing his nonsense in Munich. He wrote and said to take the children and get out. Pack a suitcase and go. I knew Gerda wouldn't be able to keep the letter to herself; by the end of the week everyone would be talking about us.

So I went straight to Fischel for bananas. He was as welcoming as ever. Good afternoon, Mrs Wollowic. Good afternoon, Mr Fischel. Dear Fischel, touching his cap like that, like he always did. I can see him now. What those animals must have done to him. I can picture it in my head. But I could never put it into words. Never. It's disgusting. He was a good man, and when he tucked those two extra bananas into my basket I knew Gerda had got to him before me. He knew what was happening.

I pulled David away from the potatoes and held onto Thelma. Bruno said he'd be waiting in London. I wanted to get everything done as soon as possible. I could have said something to Fischel. I could have said a proper goodbye but it wouldn't have made any difference. It's funny, but now he's still alive for me, somewhere back there, fiddling with his cap, sneaking bananas into my bag.

"Tell us the story again about you and Granny and uncle David," Rosalyn says.

"But I've just told it to you."

"Then tell it to us quickly," Thomas says. "Just tell us the part about the storm."

"And the banana trees," Rosalyn says.

She can't do without that happy ending.

"Granny tied me to her tummy," Thelma said. "Just like Mary ties Nelson to her back when she's polishing the floor, and she held Uncle David's hand in one hand and the big red suitcase in the other hand and we got a lift all the way to the harbour. Then we got on the big boat that was going to take us to London to meet up with Grampa."

"And did you meet Grampa, Mommy?"

Poor child, she's heard the story so many times she knows what question to ask even before the answer comes up. If I could, I would say to her: when you're a Mommy, Rossie, don't ever take your children away from anywhere. One day I'll tell her that.

"*Ja*, Mommy," says Thomas. "Did you meet Grampa?"

There was the letter from your Grampa, Thomas. There was the letter that told me everything and said I should go to South Africa instead. Your Grampa said his whole *mishpucheh* would be there to meet me. He told them we were coming; they'd take care of us.

So Thelma tells them how the boat was turned away from Portsmouth and sent to South Africa. To Africa! All I could imagine were hungry lions and big boiling pots and people with bones in their noses. I thought: is this where my children are going to land up?

"And the boat sailed all the way down Africa," Thelma says. "Past Nigeria and Angola and South West Africa."

"And Cape Town," says Thomas.

"Yes," Thelma says. "And Cape Town."

"Was it hot?" the little one asks.

"It was so hot we were stuck together," Thelma tells them.

She remembers the heat and the sweat of my skin on hers. The... Oh, God, please don't let me think about it. How can a mother do that to a child? How can she? How can she put the stink of her own flesh on her child like an animal.

"Mommy, did they have a swimming pool on the boat?"

"It wasn't that kind of boat, Tom-Tom," Thelma says.

"Was it like the Union Castle?" Thomas says.

"No, sweetheart," Thelma tells him. "It wasn't the same kind of boat you went on with Mommy and Daddy."

"And me," says the little one.

"And you, too," says Thelma.

She tells them about the friendly sailors and their white sailor suits and about the special chocolate they gave Uncle David and how he shared it with her. She tells them that I had to keep the bananas in my coat pockets until it was dark. She tells them for the millionth time that before we left the doctor said bananas were the best thing for a sick baby. So I mashed the bananas in my mouth and fed them to Thelma to keep her alive.

And then for the last week there was nothing. Thelma refused the last of my milk. She refused everything. She only wanted bananas. All that time I kept her under my clothes and she didn't make a sound. She couldn't. Without anything to eat she just kept getting smaller and smaller and nestled into me, digging a tunnel into my flesh.

"Ma, Ma. Wake up, Ma," Thelma says. "It's time to go."

Oh, God, don't say that. Don't say things like that.

"Ma, you need to get ready. Jess is here."

There's that look in her eyes that sees right through me and into the darkness of her hatred. Nobody can make me feel as hated as she can. But I love them. I do. I love them both. Her and David. He's in Canada now, just like he was on the boat, full of smiles, always happy. Making funny faces and getting people to like him. Doing little dances for the sailors. All smiles, but no children. I want to see him give someone the love that comes from seeing your children play and grow up and then being so proud you can't stop being scared. Just like the love Thelma tries to show the little ones.

My love is the love that comes from saving their lives. Seeing them dying every day and every night and singing them to sleep without saying a word. They say things like: you never showed us any affection. Why didn't you ever encourage us? You never took any interest. But I know all that. How can I tell her I still see them dying every night and still sing to them when they go to sleep even if they can't hear me?

"Granny, come on," says the little one. "Daddy's waiting in the car."

She clutches my hand tightly and pulls me up and out of the chair. *Hopala.*

"I'm coming, *ingale.* I'm coming."

Thelma says it's better if I sit in front with Jess.

The restaurant is not far and the seatbelt is so tight I need to hold it away from my chest. I want to sit in the back with the little ones. I want her to be here in the passenger seat. Mama. I want her to turn around and look at me and tell me a story about when I was a baby and she wrapped me in her arms and sang to me.

"Ma, are you okay in the front?"

Oh, my baby, little Thelma, what do you know, what questions you ask. For the thousandth time: "Of course I'm fine."

"We're nearly there," she says. "Nearly there."

Prophet Margin
Ellen Galford

You're probably too young to remember the days when time travel was still glamorous and thrilling.

Not like now.

"Collect two-for-one vouchers off the back of this cereal packet and take the family on a fun-packed adventure holiday riding with the Mongol Hordes!"

Then it's all "Hurry Along There... Stand Behind the Line... Follow the Signs to Security Strip Search... I'm Afraid There Is a Spelling Error in Your Travel Document — Please Return to Check In... We Apologise for the Nine-Hour Delay in the Departure of Flight 1066AD. This is due to Operational Difficulties in the Holy Roman Empire Sector..."

You know how it goes.

I'm probably showing my age, but I miss the way it used to be way back when temporal transport was still brand new. The facilities were simple but elegant. The atmosphere was unhurried. The staff couldn't do enough for us — courteous, efficient, genuinely keen to please. I'm sure I sound like a horrible elitist when I say this, but it was probably no coincidence that the people who made those early trips had to be very brave or very rich or very well connected.

Brave — because the technology was still quite primitive and unreliable. You might get somewhere. It might even be roughly where you wanted to go, but there was no guarantee you'd ever get back home again. Or, even if you did return, that you'd embody the same set of memories and molecules that had left home in the first place.

Rich — because every trip had to be individually programmed. It wasn't like today. There were no package tours, no economies of scale. And don't even think about the cost of the insurance.

Well connected — because you had to Be Somebody or Know Somebody. You needed character references, personal recommendations, security clearances to the nth degree.

Nobody in our family had to worry about any of these restrictions. My grandmother had headed the engineering team that ironed out the last of the technical glitches. So we didn't need to be brave, because we had absolute confidence in the process. And unlike other potential travellers we didn't need to be rich, because, thanks to Grandma's impeccable connections, we never had to pay the fare.

So from the time my brother Alex and I were old enough to toddle down the Transit Corridor, it was Access All Areas. At an age when other children were still struggling to learn their ABCs, we were being drilled in the Three Absolute Rules of Non-Intervention.

Absolute Rule 1, as students of classical literature will know, was inspired — at least in part — by the Prime Directive governing encounters with alien societies across the Universe, as codified in the Star Trek narratives. The gist is — Boggle all you

143

like at the natives' weirdness (or their equally uncanny resemblances to ourselves) but Never, Never, Never interfere with biological evolution, social development, or the general course of events. To put it even more concisely, Look But Do Not Touch.

Absolute Rule 2: Keep a Low Profile. By which is meant don't draw attention to yourself by wearing modern clothing or toting any present-day technology. Cameras or any other devices for recording and transmission — apart from your own eyes, ears and brain — are strictly forbidden.

Absolute Rule 3: Keep Your Mouth Shut.

It all made perfect sense. One doesn't have to possess a degree in quantum physics to appreciate the potential dangers of people parachuting into the past and trying to rewrite it — even with the best will in the world. We all know the one about the butterfly flappping its wings in a Costa Rican rainforest to start a chain of events that leads, incrementally yet inexorably, to a landslide in Tibet.

(Strangely enough, according to my aunt Jill, the reason Grandma first took an interest in trans-temporal logistics was so that she could go back to the 1930s and convince as many Jews as possible to get out of Europe before it was too late. My mother disagreed. She claimed it was because Grandma intended to travel even further back than that, to the late 19th century. Supposedly she wanted to warn the early Zionists that they'd better think a whole lot harder about their plans for Palestine, and that this "A Land Without People for a People Without Land" business was a real non-starter.

But since Grandma chaired the Committee that drafted the Three Absolute Rules of Non-Intervention, I think these particular legends are just a bit of wishful romancing.)

144

Imagine, then, the scandal when a member of the Chair's own family broke the rules. The guilty party, to our infinite mortification, was my brother Alex.

Of all our generation, Alex is definitely the one who inherited Grandma's intellectual firepower. But not her scientific detachment. Even as a little boy, he was highly emotional, especially concerning matters of right and wrong. He really cared about the way people treated each other.

I don't know if you can describe a six-year-old as a zealot for social justice, but there was a famous incident in the playground when he stopped a gang of miniature thugs from tormenting a newcomer. Not only did he protect the kid physically, but he made some kind of speech that put bullying completely out of fashion for the rest of that school year. As Alex got older, his English compositions always focused on questions of ethics and morality — and he became the Junior Debating Society's shining star. His only failing was that his speeches — though brilliantly argued — went on just a little too long.

My parents were convinced that he would turn out to be either a statesman or a rabbi. Needless to say, the speech he gave at his Bar Mitzvah dazzled us all. (And as to the way he read his *Haftorah* portion, what can I tell you? Fluent, expressive, and, of course, word-perfect in the Hebrew, without a hesitation or a flaw.) After that, to encourage the development of his rhetorical skills, they took us to all sorts of times and places.

As I've said, those were the glory days, with no restrictions on where you could go, as long as you were a member of the lucky chosen few. So we heard Abraham Lincoln deliver the Gettysburg Address, witnessed the first ever public performance of Shakespeare's Macbeth, and thrilled to Cicero's orations to the Roman Senate (you didn't need to know

145

Latin; it was all in the cadences).

But then, on the way home from the last of these excursions, my brother gave us the slip. My mother was furious, my father inconsolable — especially once we found the note.

"I know what I want to do with my life. Don't worry, I'll be fine. This is my destiny. Love, Alex. P.S. Please feed my tropical fish."

All sentiment aside, it is clearly not a good idea to let an idealistic and somewhat self-righteous adolescent boy run wild across the ancient world. My mother was terrified that he would catch some kind of plague or fall in with fanatics or mortally offend some despotic emperor by giving him a lecture on equality and human rights. And, most unthinkable of all, what would he do if he wanted to come home? He had no access to the technology that would pull him back.

The situation was desperate, so there was no alternative but to call upon Grandma. She had recently retired and was treating herself to what she called a busman's holiday — cruising with Charles Darwin on the Beagle.

She was, predictably, more than a little cross.

"Well, where do you think he's gone?" she asked my parents. "What are his current interests? His obsessions? He's a fourteen-year-old male. He's probably off spying on Cleopatra in her bath of asses' milk, or ogling Helen of Troy."

Not our Alex, I told them. Alex had his mind on higher things. And I should know. I was his kid sister, two years younger, so I worshipped the ground he walked on. As a result, I did a lot of eavesdropping and spying.

"Jeremiah," I told them. "He has kind of a thing about Jeremiah. Remember his Bar Mitzvah? He had to do a chapter from the Book of Jeremiah as his *Haftorah* portion. He got very excited about Jeremiah's prophecies, and what an impression they made on people in his own time and for hundreds of years after, and how accurate some of them, like the destruction of Jerusalem, turned out to be..."

"So?"

"So I think Alex wanted to go off and be Jeremiah's assistant."

"His what?"

"When he was practising for his Bar Mitzvah he used to go on and on and on about how cool it would be if he could learn some of Jeremiah's techniques for making an audience pay attention...and in exchange he could tell Jeremiah about all kinds of things that he knew were going to happen in the distant future — stuff that no rival prophet could ever find out in a million years..."

Grandma might have been out of the game, but she still had her contacts in the office. It didn't take long to make the calls.

So one minute our Alex is standing in a marketplace in old Judaea, at the side of a thundering prophet in full spate, and the next there is a flash of light and a quaver of unidentifiable energy and he finds himself walking through Gate 23 at Intertemporal Arrivals. Where my mother and father and I greet him with tears and kisses, and my grandmother greets him with a very rude gesture that hasn't been current since at least 2055.

"What about the Rules, you little no-good bandit? You, of all people, my own grandson, you serpent's tooth! You have wrought total bloody havoc with our Absolute Rules. I can't bear to think of the possible cosmological implications!"

Fortunately, after years of careful study of all the relevant literature by a committee of Hebrew and Aramaic linguists, historians and theologians, it was determined that there was no permanent damage done. The only slight residual effect may have been a tradition regarding the conveyance of certain holy men up to heaven by miraculous and unconventional means. And even this, by the late 1900s, had largely been subsumed into a set of cultic theories regarding the intervention of extraterrestrial aliens upon human affairs.

But the Absolute Rules of Time Travel never really recovered from the affront.

And these days, of course, they are are virtually obsolete. It doesn't matter how rash or stupid or insensitive you are. As long as you can pay for the ticket, you go. Thanks to the development of The Bubble (as the current technology is popularly known) contact with the locals has long since become physically impossible. They can't see or hear or smell or sense us. Every aspect of every trip is rigidly controlled. Obviously this is safer for all parties, but as far as I'm concerned, it's taken the edge off, killed all the danger and romance.

I know I should celebrate the fact that time-travel, in however sanitised a form, is now accessible to all. And the range of options and package tours increases daily. There's almost nowhere (and no when) where you can't go.

With one exception.

Don't even think about visiting the Middle East during the formative periods of the three great Abrahamic religions. I'm sure we'd all love to know how closely the actual events on the ground actually match up to the reports enshrined in the relevant sacred books, but there is no way anybody will get the chance to find out. Imagine the fallout. To borrow the slang of an earlier era, "Just don't go there."

Our Alex did, of course. But whatever he saw there, my grandmother made him promise not to tell. So he's not saying. Nobody messes with Grandma.

Psychoanalysis Changed My Life
Amy Bloom

For three weeks, four days a week, Marianne told her dreams to Dr. Zurmer. Fat, naked women handed her bouquets of tiger lilies; incomprehensible signs and directories punctuated silent grey corridors; bodiless penises spewed azalea blossoms in great pink and purple arcs. She also talked about her marriage, her divorce, and her parents. Behind her, Dr. Zurmer nodded and took notes and occasionally slipped her knotted, elderly feet out of elegant black velvet flats, wiggling her toes until she could feel her blood begin to move. Marianne could hear her even and attentive breathing, could hear the occasional light scratch of her cigar-like fountain pen.

At the end of another long dream, in which Marianne's father frantically attempted to reach Marianne through steadily drifting petals, Dr. Zurmer put down her pen.

"Why don't you sit up, Dr. Loewe?"

Marianne didn't move, still thinking of the soft drifts and the few white petals that had clung to her father's beard as he struggled toward her. Dr. Zurmer thought she had shocked her patient into immobility.

"After all, there are two of us in the room. Why should we pretend that only one of us is real, that only one of us is present?"

Marianne sat up.

"All these white flower dreams," Dr. Zurmer said, "what are they about?"

"I'm sure they're about my mother. I don't know if you remember, my mother's name was Lily. And she was like a white flower, thin, pale, graceful. Just wafting around, not a solid person at all. Just a little bit of everything, you know, real estate, house painting, for a while she read tea leaves in some fake Gypsy restaurant. I mean, now she's a businesswoman, but then... My father was the stable one, but she drove him away."

Dr. Zurmer said, "He was stable, but he disappeared. You say she was 'wafting around,' but she never left you. And she always made a living, yes?"

"He didn't disappear. My mother was having an affair, one of many, I'm sure, she was such a fucking belle of the ball, and he couldn't stand it and he left." Marianne was glad that she could say "fucking".

"It's understandable that he would choose to end the marriage. Not everyone would, but it's understandable. But why did he stop seeing you?"

"He didn't really have much choice. She got custody somehow, and then he moved to California for his work. I went to California once, for about a week, but then, I don't know, he remarried, and then he died in a car accident." Marianne started to cry and wished she were back on the couch, invisible.

"How old were you when you went to California?"

"Nine."

"How did you get there?"

"My mother took me by plane."

"Your mother took you by plane to California so you could visit your father?"

"Sometimes she was overprotective. I remember he said

151

that when I was old enough to take the plane by myself I could come out there. I thought nine was old enough, but my mother took me."

"Of course. Why would you send a nine-year-old three thousand miles away by herself, unless it was an emergency?"

"Lots of people do."

"Lots of people behave selfishly and irresponsibly. It doesn't seem that your father thought nine was really old enough either. He, however, was willing to wait another year or two before you saw each other."

"It wasn't like that."

"I think it was. You are almost forty now. I am almost eighty-five. We are not going to have time for a long analysis, Dr. Loewe, which is just as well. I will tell you what I see, when I see something, but you have to be willing to look. Your mother knew how important your father was to you, and even though your father had left her, she was willing to take the time and money to make sure that you saw him, even in the face of his indifference. You must think about why you need your father to be the hero of this story. Tomorrow, yes?"

Marianne went home, less happy than she had been the first time they met. Three weeks ago, walking into that grey-carpeted waiting room, with its two black-and-white Sierra Club photographs and the dusty mahogany coffee table offering only last week's *Paris-Match* and last year's *New Yorkers*, Marianne knew that she was in sure and authentic hands. Despite an unexpected penchant for bright, bulky sweaters, made charming and European by carefully embroidered flowers on the pockets, Dr. Zurmer was just what Marianne had hoped for.

On Tuesday, Dr. Zurmer interrupted Marianne's memory of her grandfather shaving with an old-fashioned straight razor to tell her that beige was not her colour. "Beige is for redheads, for certain blondes. Not for you. My hair was the same colour fifty years ago. *Chatin*. Ahh, chestnut. A lovely colour, even with the grey. You would look very nice in green, all different greens, like spring leaves. Maybe a ring or a bracelet, as well, to call attention to your pretty hands."

Marianne looked at Dr. Zurmer, and Dr. Zurmer smiled back.

"We must stop for today. Tomorrow, Dr. Loewe."

Marianne went home and fed her cat, and as she put on her navy bathrobe and her backless slippers, she watched herself in the mirror.

During the next week's sessions, Dr. Zurmer gave Marianne the name of a good masseuse, an expert hair colourist, and a store that specialised in narrow-width Swiss shoes, which turned out to be perfect for Marianne's feet and sensibilities. At the end of Thursday's session, Dr. Zurmer suggested that Marianne focus less on the past and more on the present.

"Your mother invites you to her beachhouse every weekend, Dr. Loewe. Why not go? I don't think she wants to devour you or humiliate you. I think she wants to show off her brilliant daughter to her friends and she wants you to appreciate the life she's made for herself — beachhouse and catering business and so on. This is no small potatoes for a woman of her background, for the delicate flower you say she is. Life is short, Dr. Loewe. Go visit your mother and see what is really there. At the very worst, you will have escaped this dreadful heat and you will return to tell me that my notions are all wet."

Charmed by Dr. Zurmer's archaic Americanisms and the vision of herself and her mother walking on the beach at sunset, their identical short, strong legs and narrow feet skimming through the sand, Marianne rose to leave, not waiting for Dr. Zurmer's dismissal.

Dr. Zurmer began to rise and could not. Her head fell forward, and her half-moon glasses, which made her look so severe and so kind, landed on the floor.

Marianne crouched beside Dr. Zurmer's chair and put just her fingertips on Dr. Zurmer's shoulder. Dr. Zurmer did not lift her head.

"Please take me home. I am not well."

"Should I call your doctor? Or an ambulance? They can bring you to the hospital."

"I am not going to a hospital. Please take me home." Dr. Zurmer raised her head, and without her glasses she looked extremely vulnerable and reptilian, an ancient turtle, arrogant in its longevity, resigned to its fate.

Terrified, Marianne drove Dr. Zurmer home, regretting the Kleenex and Health Bar wrappers in the backseat, where Dr. Zurmer lay, pain dampening and distorting the matt, powdery surface of her fine old skin. When they approached a small Spanish-style house with ivy reaching up to the red tile roof and slightly weedy marigolds lining the front walk, Dr. Zurmer indicated that Marianne should pull into the driveway. Marianne could not imagine carrying Dr. Zurmer up the walk, although she was probably capable of lifting her, but she didn't think Dr. Zurmer could make the hundred yards on her own.

"Is someone home? I can go let them know that you're here, and they can give us a hand."

Dr. Zurmer nodded twice, and her head sagged back against the seat.

A thin old man, shorter than Marianne and leaning hard on a rubber-tipped cane, opened the door. Marianne explained what had happened, even mentioning that she was Dr. Zurmer's patient, which was a weird and embarrassing thing to have to say to the man who was obviously her analyst's husband. He nodded and followed Marianne out to the car. It was clear to Marianne that this little old man was in no position to carry his wife to the house, and that she, Marianne, would have to stick around for a few more minutes and take Dr. Zurmer in, probably to her bedroom, perhaps to her bathroom, which was not a pleasant thought.

"Otto," was all Dr. Zurmer said.

They spoke softly in Russian, and Marianne gently pulled Dr. Zurmer from the backseat, handing her briefcase to the husband, half carrying, half dragging Dr. Zurmer up the walk under his critical, anxious eye. Dr. Zurmer's husband seemed not to speak English, or not to speak to people other than his wife.

Marianne was so focused on not dropping Dr. Zurmer and following Mr. or Dr. Zurmer's hand signals that she barely saw her analyst's house, although she had wondered about it, with occasional, pleasurable intensity, in the last three weeks. Dr. Zurmer slipped out of Marianne's arms onto a large bed covered with a white lace spread and said thank you and goodbye. Marianne, who had not wanted to come and had not wanted to stay, felt that this was a little abrupt, even ungracious, but she was polite and said it was no trouble and that she would find her own way out so that they would not be disturbed. The old man had lain down next to his wife and was wiping her damp face with his handkerchief.

Marianne walked down the narrow, turning staircase, noticing the scratched brass rods that anchored the faded green carpeting, and looking into the faces in the framed photographs that dotted the wall beside her like dark windows. Two skinny boys in baggy dark trunks are building a huge, turreted sandcastle trimmed with seashells, twigs, and the remains of horseshoe crabs, surrounded by a moat that reaches up to the knees of a younger, taller Otto Zurmer. In another, the two skinny boys are now skinny teenagers sitting on a stone wall, back to back like bookends, in matching sunglasses, matching bare chests, and matching fearless and immortal grins.

Marianne was conscious of lingering, of trespassing, in fact, and she only took one quick look at the photograph that interested her the most. Dr. Zurmer, whose first name, Anya, Marianne had read on the brass plaque of her office door, is sitting, in a velvet armchair, legs stretched sideways and crossed at the slender white silk ankles. She cannot be more than twenty, and she looks pampered, with her lace-trimmed dress and carefully curled hair, and she looks beautiful; she peers uncertainly at the viewer, eager and afraid.

Marianne spent the next week working harder on the book she was trying to write, staking the tomato plants in her small yard, and getting her hair coloured. It came out eye-catching and rich, the colour of fine luggage, the colour of expensive brandy, the kind drunk only by handsome old men sitting in wing armchairs by their early evening fires. Marianne was tempted to wear a scarf until the colour faded, but she could not bear to cover it up, and at night she fanned it out on her pillow and admired what she could see of the fine, gleaming strands.

She waited to hear from Dr. Zurmer and decided that if she didn't get word from her by Friday, she would leave a message with the answering service. On Friday, Dr. Zurmer called. She told Marianne that she was not yet well enough to return to the office but could see her for a session at home. She did not ask Marianne how she felt about meeting with her therapist, in her therapist's home, with little Dr./Mr. Zurmer running in and out, she simply inquired whether Monday at nine would suit her. That was their usual time, and

Marianne said yes and hung up the phone quickly so as not to tire Dr. Zurmer, who sounded terrible.

Dr. Zurmer's husband let Marianne in silently, but when she was fully through the door he took her hand in both of his and thanked her, in perfectly good English.

"Please call me Otto," he said. His smile was very kind, and Marianne said her name and was pleased with them both.

Dr. Zurmer sat in bed, propped up by dozens of large and small Battenberg lace pillows, her silver hair brushed, neat and sleek as mink. She wore a remarkably businesslike grey satin bed jacket. Marianne couldn't tell if Dr. Zurmer's face was slightly longer and looser than before or if she had forgotten, in a week, exactly what Dr. Zurmer looked like.

"I feel much better today. A very tiny stroke, my doctor said. And no harm done, apparently. Thank you, Dr. Loewe. So, I will lie down during our sessions and you will sit up."

Marianne began by telling Dr. Zurmer her latest flower dream but wrapped it up quickly in order to talk about the photograph of Dr. Zurmer, not mentioning the boys; and she sat back in the little brocade chair, looking at the ceiling, in order to talk about the dislocating, fascinating oddness of being in Dr. Zurmer's house. Dr. Zurmer smiled, shaking her head sympathetically, and fell asleep. Marianne sat quietly, only a little insulted, and watched Dr. Zurmer breathe. At her elbow was a mahogany dresser laid over with embroidered, crocheted runners, four small photographs in silver frames and three perfume bottles of striped Murano glass sitting on top. The little gold-tipped bottles were almost empty. One photograph, as Marianne expected, shows the two young men from the stone wall and the beach, a good bit older, both in suits. They are clearly at a wedding, with linen-covered tables and gladioli behind them, although there is no bride in sight. Another shows Dr. Zurmer and Otto, their arms around each other, in front of the lighthouse at Gay Head, and the picture is not unlike one of Marianne and her ex-husband, at that same spot, during the brief, good time of their marriage. The other two photographs are of a dark-skinned woman in a bathrobe, holding what must he a baby wrapped in a blue and white blanket, and finally, a very little boy with black curls, jug ears, and the same slightly slant, long-lashed eyes as the woman.

As Marianne reached the front door, Otto clumped toward her.

"Tea?" he said, waving his cane toward the back of the house.

Marianne said no and went home to look up the phone numbers of other psychoanalysts.

On Thursday, Otto called. "Please come today," he said. "She wants to see you."

Marianne had already set up a consultation with another analyst, a middle-aged man with a good reputation and an office overlooking the river, but she went.

Dr. Zurmer was sitting up again, her bed jacket open over a flannel nightgown and her hair tufted in downy silver puffs. She stretched out her hand for Marianne's and held onto it as Marianne sat down, much closer than planned.

"It seems that I am not well enough to be your analyst after all. But I don't think we should let that stop us from enjoying each other's company, do you? You come and visit, and we'll have tea."

Marianne could not imagine why Dr. Zurmer wanted her to visit.

"Why not? You're smart, a very kind person, you have a wonderful imagination and sense of humour — I see that in

158

your dreams — why shouldn't I want you to visit me? Otto will bring us tea. Sit."

Over pale green tea swarming with brown bits of leaf, Marianne and Dr. Zurmer smiled at each other. "I was very interested in the photographs on your dresser," Marianne said.

"What about them interests you?"

"This is just a visit, remember? Tea and conversation."

Dr. Zurmer pretended to slap her own wrist and smiled broadly at Marianne, her cheeks folding up like silk ruching.

"Touché," she said. "Bring the photos over here, please. And there's an album in the magazine rack there.

"Oh, look at this, little Alexei. Everyone has these bathtub photographs tucked away. And this is Alexei in Cub Scouts, I think that lasted for six months. He loved the uniform, but he was not, not Scout material. And this is him with his brother, Robert. You saw some of these on the wall, I think. At Martha's Vineyard. We used to stay at a little farmhouse, two bedrooms and a tiny kitchen. Friends of Otto's lent it to us every summer. Otto designed their house, the big house in the background here, and their house, I forget, in the suburbs of Boston. We were the house pets, but it was wonderful for the children. This is Robert's college graduation. I can't remember what all the armbands represent, he protested everything. Unfortunately for him, we were liberals, so it was difficult to disturb us. He did become a banker, there was that. And here is Alexei graduating, no armbands, just the hair. But it was such beautiful hair, I wanted him to keep it long, I thought he looked like Apollo. And here are the wedding pictures, Alexei and his wife, Naria. Lebanese. They met in graduate school. And this is my only grandson, Lee. As beautiful as the day. As good as he is beautiful. Very bright child. Alexei is a wonderful father, father and mother both. This big

one is Lee last year, on his fourth birthday. That's his favourite
bear, I don't remember now, the train station name."

"Paddington. He's lovely. Lee is just lovely."

"Naria left them almost two years ago. She has a narcissistic personality disorder. She simply could not mother. People
cannot do what they are not equipped to do. So, she's gone,
back to Lebanon. Also, very self-destructive, to return to a
place like Lebanon, divorced, a mother, clearly not a virgin.
She will care for her father, in his home, for the rest of her
life. Who can say? Perhaps that was her wish."

Dr. Zurmer said "narcissistic personality disorder" the way
you'd say "terminal cancer," and Marianne nodded, understanding that Naria was gone from this earth.

"And this is a picture Alexei took of me and Otto two
years ago. Those two lovers, the gods made them into trees,
or bushes? Philomena? So that they might never part. We
look like that, yes? Already beginning to merge with the
earth."

Dr. Zurmer lay back, and the album slid between them.
"I cannot really speak of loving him anymore. Does one
love the brain, or the heart? Does one appreciate one's
blood! We have kept each other from the worst loneliness,
and we listen to each other. We don't say anything very
interesting anymore, we talk of Lee, of Alexei, we remember Robert ..."

Marianne waited for the terrible story.

"He died in a car accident, right after the wedding. I am
still grieving and I am still angry. He was drinking too much,
that was something he did. Alexei, never. My bad Russian
genes. He left nothing behind, an apartment full of junk, a job
he disliked, debts. I thought perhaps a pregnant girlfriend
would emerge, but that didn't happen. I would have made it
so, if I could have. I have to rest, my dear."

Dr. Zurmer sank back into her pillows and asked Marianne to go into the bottom drawer of the mahogany dresser. Marianne brought her the only thing in it, a bolt of green satin, thick and cool, rippling in her hands like something alive. Dr. Zurmer tied it around her waist, turning Marianne's white shirt and khaki slacks into something dashing, exotic, and slightly, delightfully androgynous.

"Just so. When you leave, please say goodbye to Otto. He likes you so much. 'Such a luffly girl,'" she said, mimicking Otto's accent, which was, if anything, less noticeable, less guttural, than her own. "If he's not in the kitchen, just wait a minute. He's probably getting the newspaper, going for his constitutional. Be well, Marianne. Come again soon."

The man sitting at the kitchen table was so clearly the slightly bigger boy from the photographs, the bearded groom, that Marianne smiled at him familiarly, filled with tenderness and receptivity, as though her pores were steaming open. He stared back at her and then, with great, courtly gestures, folded the newspaper and slid it behind the toaster.

"You must be Marianne."

"Yes. I just wanted to say goodbye to your father, I'm on my way home," she said.

"That will please him. I'm Alex Zurmer. I don't know where Pop is." He looked at her again, at her deep brown eyes and long neck, his own sweet baby giraffe, and watched her blunt, bony fingers playing with the fringe of the glimmering green sash. Alex shrugged, lifting his palms heavenward, as awestruck and graceful as Noah, knowing that he had been selected for survival and the arrival of doves. He watched Marianne's restless, slightly bitten fingers twisting in and out of the thick tasseled ends, and he could feel them touching his face, lifting his hair.

161

"Let's have tea while we wait. Marianne," he said, and he rose to pull out her chair, and she very deliberately laid her hand next to his on the back of the chair.

"Let's," said Marianne. "Let's put out a few cookies too. If you use loose tea, I'll read the leaves."

The Contributors

Amy Bloom is the author of two novels, two short story collections and a book of essays. She teaches at Yale University in Connecticut.

Ellen Galford has published four novels; *Moll Cutpurse: Her True History, The Fires of Bride, Queendom Come,* and *The Dyke and the Dybbuk,* which received a 1994 Lambda Award for Gay and Lesbian Literature. She has also contributed short stories to various anthologies. She lives in Scotland, where she is currently studying Yiddish. Her first Yiddish poem has recently been put to music and recorded on CD by the Edinburgh-based Yiddish Song Project.

Tania Hershman (www.taniahershman.com) is a former science journalist living in Jerusalem, Israel. Her award-winning short stories have been published in print and online in literary magazines and broadcast on BBC Radio 4. Tania is European regional winner of the 2008 Commonwealth Broadcasting Association short story competition. She is founder and editor of The Short Review (www.theshortreview.com), a site dedicated to reviewing short story collections.Tania's own first collection, *The White Road and Other Stories* (www.thewhiteroadandotherstories.com), is published by Salt Publishing.

Zvi Jagendorf was born in Vienna 1936. He read English at Oxford and moved to Israel in 1958 to teach at the Hebrew University. He taught in the English and Theatre departments, acted in Hebrew and English theatre, worked as a radio journalist, theatre critic and was visiting lecturer at Tel Aviv and Haifa Universities. His prize-winning comic novel about refugees in England *Wolfy and the Strudelbakers* (Dewi Lewis) has been translated into Hebrew and German.

Anne Joseph is a freelance feature writer and editor (www.annejoseph.co.uk). She previously worked for several years as submissions editor for Haus Publishing. Her book, *From the Edge* *of the World* (2003, Vallentine Mitchell), is a collection of letters and stories written by Jewish refugees.

Etgar Keret is one of the leading voices in Israeli literature and cinema. His books have been published in 25 different languages to both critical acclaim and success. The movie *Jellyfish*, codirected by Keret and Shira Geffen, won the Camera d'Or prize for best first feature in the 2007 Cannes festival.

Nicole Krauss is the author of the international bestseller, *The History of Love*, which won France's Prix du Meilleur Livre Étranger and Amazon's #1 Book of the Year, and was shortlisted for the Orange, Médicis, and Femina prizes. Her first novel, *Man Walks Into a Room*, was a finalist for the Los Angeles Times Book of the Year. Her fiction has been published in *The New Yorker*, *Harper's*, *Esquire*, and *Best American Short Stories*. In 2007 she was selected as one of Granta's Best Young American Novelists. Her books have been translated into more than thirty languages.

Shaun Levin is the author of *A Year of Two Summers* (Five Leaves, 2005), *Seven Sweet Things* (bluechrome, 2003) and most recently *Isaac Rosenberg's Journey to Arras: A Meditation* (Cecil Woolf, 2008). His work appears in anthologies as diverse as *Between Men*, *Modern South African Stories*, *Boyfriends from Hell*, and *Desperate Remedies*. Shaun is the editor of *Chroma: A Queer Literary and Arts Journal*.

Karen Maitland lives in Lincoln. She writes fiction and nonfiction, including co-writing a number of cross-cultural books. Her first novel, *The White Room*, was shortlisted for The Authors' Club Best First Novel Award. Her medieval thriller, *Company of Liars*, was published in 2008, by Penguin (UK) and Bantam Dell (USA). Karen's *The Owl Killers* is published in March 2009.

Jon McGregor was born in Bermuda in 1976, grew up in Norfolk, and now lives in Nottingham with his wife and daughter. His first novel, *If Nobody Speaks of Remarkable Things*, was awarded the 2003 Betty Trask Prize, longlisted for the 2002 Man Booker Prize, and shortlisted for the Commonwealth Writers' Prize for Best First Book, the Times Young Writer Award, and the Author's Club Best First Novel Award. His latest book, *So Many Ways to Begin*, was longlisted for the 2006 Man Booker Prize.

Eshkol Nevo was born in Jerusalem in 1971 and now lives in Ranana, Israel. He studied copywriting at Triza Granot School and Psychology at Tel Aviv University. Author of the award winning novel *Homesick*, his second novel *World Cup Wishes* is a number one best seller in Israel. He runs creative writing workshops as well as teaching creative writing at Sam Spiegel Film and Television School and Tel Aviv University. Nevo has also published a collection of short stories and a work of non-fiction.

Anne Sebba read history at London University and her first job was at the BBC World Service in the Arabic Section. She worked at Reuters as a foreign correspondent in London and Rome before moving to New York in 1979. She has written eight books — *Jennie Churchill: Winston's American Mother* is her latest — as well as several introductions to republished classics and short stories. She is a trustee of two charities, PEN, the Writers' Organisation, and YAD, dedicated to bringing Israelis and Arabs together through the arts.

Ali Smith was born in Inverness in 1962 and lives in Cambridge. She is the author of *Free Love*, *Like*, *Hotel World*, *Other Stories and Other Stories*, *The Whole Story and Other Stories*, *The Accidental* and *Girl Meets Boy*. Her most recent book is *The First Person and Other Stories*, published in 2008.

Michelene Wandor is a poet, playwright and fiction writer. (www.mwandor.co.uk). Her recent poetry collections, *Musica Transalpina* and *Music of the Prophets* contain narrative poems about the Jews in England. She has written two books about creative writing: *The Author is Not Dead, merely Somewhere Else* and *The Art of Writing Drama*. She holds a Royal Literary Fund Fellowship.

Jonathan Wilson is the author of seven books: the novels *The Hiding Room* and *A Palestine Affair,* a finalist for the 2004 National Jewish Book Award, two collections of short stories *Schoom* and *An Ambulance is on the Way: Stories of Men in Trouble*, two critical works on the fiction of Saul Bellow and most recently a biography, *Marc Chagall*, runnerup for the 2007 National Jewish Book Award. His work has appeared in *The New Yorker*, *The New York Times Magazine* and *Best American Short Stories*, among other publications,

165

and he has received a Guggenheim Fellowship. He is Fletcher Professor of Rhetoric and Debate, Professor of English and Director of the Center for the Humanities at Tufts University.

Tamar Yellin's first novel, *The Genizah at the House of Shepher*, received the Ribalow Prize 2006 and the Rohr Prize 2007 and was shortlisted for the Wingate Prize. Her collection, *Kafka in Brontëland and other stories*, was a finalist for the Edge Hill Prize and received the Reform Judaism Prize 2006. *Tales of the Ten Lost Tribes* appeared in September 2008.

Richard Zimler's novels have been published in more than twenty languages. His works of historical fiction include The *Last Kabbalist of Lisbon, Hunting Midnight, Guardian of the Dawn* and *The Seventh Gate*. He recently edited *The Children's Hours*, an anthology of short stories for which all the writers' royalties are going directly to Save the Children. He can be reached via his website: www.zimler.com.

Fives Leaves Publications gratefully acknowledges permission to reprint the following works

Acknowledgments

Without the following people's efficiency, advice and assistance *The Sea of Azov* would never have been produced.

Tracy Bohan and Luke Ingram from The Wylie Agency.
Jane Cramb @ Pan Macmillan, London.
James Libson for legal guidance.
Anne Sebba.
Martine Halban.
Helen Bender.
Administrative support from WJR office staff.
Geraldine D'Amico, Director, Jewish Book Week.
Aloma Halter.
Ardyn Halter.
Hilla Megged and Pat Dimet @ ITHL (The Institute for the Translation of Hebrew Literature).
Sondra Silverston, translator for Eshkol Nevo.
Linda Rosenblatt, Vice-Chair of WJR. Her professionalism and dedication to WJR are truly admirable.

And lastly, sincere thanks to Ross Bradshaw, Five Leaves Publications and to all the contributing authors who donated their work and time free of charge in support of this book.